KILLER SPECIES
menace from the deep

KILLER SPECIES
menace from the deep

Michael P. Spradlin

SCHOLASTIC INC.

No part of this publication may be reproduced, stored in a
retrieval system, or transmitted in any form or by any means,
electronic, mechanical, photocopying, recording, or otherwise,
without written permission of the publisher. For information
regarding permission, write to Scholastic Inc., Attention:
Permissions Department, 557 Broadway, New York, NY 10012.

ISBN 978-0-545-50671-7

12 11 10 9 8 7 6 5 4 3 2   13 14 15 16 17 18/0

Printed in the U.S.A.   40
First printing, July 2013

The display type was set in Badhouse Light.
The text type was set in Apollo MT.
Book design by Nina Goffi

To my son, Mick.
Animal lover and the finest man I know.

KILLER SPECIES

menace from the deep

Prologue
Everglades National Park
August

THE BOAT SLID SILENTLY ACROSS THE SURFACE OF THE water. At the stern the man turned the tiller to the left on the nearly silent electric motor. The craft responded instantly and he pointed the bow toward a bank of mangrove trees rising up out of the swamp. After thirty yards, he switched the motor off and the boat floated to a stop, the trees another twenty yards away. He flipped on his infrared night-vision goggles and studied the trees for heat signatures. Scanning from the far left of the tree line, he saw nothing. Then, there it was, a slight movement in the branches of a tree to his right.

The snake was at least twenty to twenty-five feet long. Though reptiles are cold-blooded, it still gave off some residual heat from the sunlight it absorbed during the day. Besides, the night-vision goggles the man wore were the most advanced in the world. They could detect a heat signature from a burned-out match for three minutes after the flame died. Unlike a warm-blooded mammal, which would show up as bright red in the view-screen, the snake appeared as a light blue image, twisted around the branches of the tree.

He picked up a tablet computer from the console in front of him, touching an icon on the screen. Near the bow of the thirty-foot craft sat two metal cages fastened to the port and starboard sides. Receiving a signal from the tablet, the electronically controlled doors on the cages rose up, and two of his greatest creations, representing years of work, slithered over the sides of the boat and slipped into the water.

Were it daytime, and someone could see the creatures swimming toward the trees, they would look like ordinary alligators. But only at first glance. Both were close to twelve feet long and moved effortlessly through the water. They had the familiar snout and scaly skin with bony ridges along the back.

But a biologist or park ranger or anyone more familiar with the species would immediately notice that these two were different. For one thing, most of their bodies rode above the surface of the water rather than below. This was because their lungs were not like those of a normal alligator and were more similar to those found in birds, their distant evolutionary relatives. These lungs held more air, making them more buoyant. When swimming, they floated, though they were still capable of diving beneath the water's surface and holding their breath for a long time.

The eyes were different as well: less reptilian, sitting higher on the bony structure of the face, and more similar to those one would find on a bird of prey, like a hawk or eagle. These alligators possessed superior vision and could even see well beneath the water.

But it was what would happen once they left the water that would send a sense of complete and utter awe through anyone who witnessed it.

The two swimming reptiles hesitated for a moment. This was the most critical part of the man's experiment, and he held his breath. Another difference between these creatures and a normal alligator was in their elongated necks. Again, it was similar to a bird's, and they could lift it out of the water, their heads able to move in any direction.

"Come on, my pets," he whispered, his pulse racing. With no movement by his creations, thoughts of failure entered his mind. In the lab tests they almost immediately zeroed in on their prey. He believed he'd done an adequate job of re-creating the conditions they would face once released into the swamp. But here in the wild, perhaps there were just too many competing odors. His gene splicing and DNA sequencing, which theoretically gave them an enhanced sense of smell, had not accounted for the pungent odors of the swamp.

They floated motionless in the water, moving their heads back and forth. Nothing. He was devastated. He would need to return his specimens to his . . . Wait. Something happened. They lowered their heads and swam powerfully toward the trees.

The man would not allow himself to grow too excited yet. The next few minutes would reveal whether his grand experiment to eradicate the Everglades of invasive species would have any chance of working. He found his breath coming in ragged gasps. It was going to work.

And soon the entire world would see it firsthand.

He called these specially altered alligators *Pterogators*, a name chosen for a specific reason, and soon the whole world would understand why. They reached the bank of trees and silently exited the water. He switched his goggles from infrared to normal night vision to get a clearer view of the events taking place. He pushed another button on the tablet to record the scene before him through his view-screen.

The snake in the tree, fifteen feet above the ground, sensed no danger yet. The two Pterogators split up, each moving toward the trunk of the tree where the python rested in the branches above them. They displayed another difference from a normal gator as they walked. These beasts walked on longer legs, each with a more flexible joint in the middle, leading to clawed feet. And claws that were sharper, and far deadlier, than those of regular alligators, more closely resembling the talons one would find on a bird of prey.

In the boat, the man couldn't suppress a grin. It was going better than he could have imagined. He nearly squealed with delight as they walked across the sand and climbed the trees, using their clawed feet and jointed legs to pull themselves onto the lower branches. They pushed themselves ever upward, using their tails for support. With their improved limbs, they were each six feet above the python in a few seconds.

The snake sensed danger, raising its head and flicking its tongue, seeking whatever was out there in the dark. It was at a disadvantage at night. It normally fed on warm-blooded mammals, but these enhanced reptiles now stalking it were cold-blooded. They stored heat from the sun, like reptiles, but the man's changes to their DNA made sure their bodies would not give off enough heat to alert their primary prey. The snake was as good as blind. Its absorbed heat would give it the energy to last through the evening. But it would be sluggish and less aggressive in the dark.

The python moved its head back and forth, slithering

down the tree trunk. But it was too late. The Pterogators leapt from their perches in the nearby trees. As they jumped they spread all four legs and a flap of skin opened, connected to their bodies, just above their knee joints. It allowed them to glide from branch to branch, much like their reptilian ancestors, the archosaurs, navigated the canopy of the Cretaceous forest millions of years ago.

They fell upon the snake, their rakish claws carving into the python. The snake turned and struck the closest beast, trying desperately to sink its fangs into the hard, scaly skin. It had no effect. The python struck again and again but could not find purchase on the creatures about to destroy it.

The first bites from the genetically superior creatures were devastating. They bit down with a force equivalent to a one-thousand-pound sledgehammer crushing a watermelon, killing the snake instantly. Though it was already dead, the nerves and muscles throughout its body continued to twitch. The gators continued their work, and in less than two minutes the snake was a mass of twisted scales and flesh.

In the boat, the man pumped his fist in quiet glee. Overjoyed at his success, he pushed another button on the tablet and a homing beacon attached to the cages at the bow started pulsating. The signal was transmitted to collars attached to his pets. They hurried across the sand and silently entered the water. In a few minutes they reached the boat and crawled back into their cages. The doors slid shut.

The man smiled. His first field test was a complete success. At last he had discovered the answer to the Burmese pythons and the boa constrictors destroying his beloved Everglades. For years he had used his status and position in Florida to seek a solution through the government, private foundations, and his own organization, but his suggestions always fell on deaf ears.

Luckily, he had access to resources and the scientific knowledge to bring his plan to reality. He would save the delicate ecological balance of the Everglades. Soon he would prove that his methods were not in vain. He would go down in history with men like John James Audubon, John Muir, and Henry David Thoreau. Men who devoted their lives to saving the land and its creatures.

Soon the world would know his name.

Not yet. But soon.

1

Florida City, Florida
Six Months Later

EITHER THE PICKUP TRUCK NEEDED NEW SHOCKS OR Florida City needed new roads. Emmet Doyle couldn't decide which. A few miles back they'd stopped at a fast-food restaurant, and for the third time in the last ten minutes, one of his fries went flying in the air as the truck bounced across another pothole.

"Geez, Dad," he said. "Ever thought about defensive driving? Maybe actually avoiding a moon crater once in a while?" The fry was still in midair when Apollo, the black, fluffy-faced mutt seated next to Emmet, snatched it in his mouth. It was like having a canine vacuum cleaner. His concentration on the bag of fries in Emmet's hand was unwavering. He sat poised, nearly trembling, waiting for another piece of fried potatoey goodness to escape its unjust captivity.

"Sorry," Emmet's dad said. "Probably should have gotten the shocks replaced before we left Montana."

"Probably," Emmet muttered, looking out the window. He was twelve and moving for the fourth time in six years. His dad was most recently posted to Montana for just over a year, not long after Emmet's mom died. Emmet liked Montana. So far, he didn't like Florida. He liked the mountains and the fresh air. It was better than any of the other places they'd lived over the last few years, even though he missed his mom. She would have loved it there. In Florida it was hot and humid, and everything smelled like mildew.

"It smells like swamp here," he muttered.

"Well, we are in the Everglades, which are known for their swampiness," his dad said, trying hard to make it sound funny and cheerful. Emmet sighed. His dad was so Captain Obvious sometimes.

"Don't worry, Emmet. You'll get used to the smell. Eventually, nasal fatigue will set in and you won't even notice it."

"I doubt that," Emmet said quietly. He glanced out the window, his hand lowering the bag of fries so it rested on the seat. Apollo didn't hesitate. He grabbed a mouthful and swallowed them in a single gulp. Emmet didn't care. He wasn't hungry anymore. This was the second move without his mom, and it made him really miss her. They'd packed all of their important possessions into the truck, and a moving van was bringing the rest. But Emmet knew that with each move they would leave a little bit more of her behind.

She had gotten sick and died. It happened fast, so suddenly she'd been gone in a matter of months. It just was. The truck bounced again, and Emmet thought maybe they all needed shock absorbers. Not just the truck, but him and his dad, and even Apollo. After Emmet's mom died, Apollo would wake up in his room every morning and search the house for her. Even when they moved to Montana, he still bounded around the house like he expected to find her in the next room. Emmet wondered how long it was before dogs forgot people. Or if they even did.

The thing of it was, his mom would have gotten the shocks fixed at the auto-repair shop before they'd left. She would have organized the trip and all the details, just like she'd done all the previous times. His mom would have told him she knew how hard it was to move, but that he needed to look for the good in things. His father's work was very important, she would have said. He was a scientist who was helping to save the environment and endangered animals.

Emmet understood that. He was proud of it, even. But he quickly grew sick of moving and of always being the new kid in school. In Montana, he'd learned to ski and snowboard, and was just starting to make friends. Once Emmet asked his mom why his dad couldn't just go where he was needed, like he was on a business trip, and the two of them could stay in one place. "Because," his mom said, "you can't save endangered species overnight or in two weeks. It takes a lot of time and effort for your father to get his programs up and running. We need to be with him. We need to be a family."

But the thing was, whenever they moved to where his dad was posted, they seldom saw him anyway. He was always out in the field. Emmet wanted to stay in one place and go to school and act like a normal kid for a change.

"Look," his dad said. "I know you didn't want to move. And it would have . . . been so much . . ." His dad let the words trail off. He was trying hard. Emmet knew he was making an effort. His dad tried to explain — even with Mom gone, he couldn't give up his job. Keeping food on the table meant they were going to have to move. He was sorry, but that was how it was.

So they packed up the truck and five days later they were in Florida City, smelling swamp odors. Emmet didn't like driving in complete silence. But his dad lived inside his own head a lot and wasn't a great conversationalist. One of the most preeminent men in his field, but not much for small talk. He passed some of the hours listening to music, but even that grew old after a while. They stayed at campgrounds along the way because they never knew how far they would drive each day, and most hotels wouldn't allow dogs. That wasn't so bad. Emmet liked camping out. But after a long, quiet trip, he was hot, tired, and cranky.

The headquarters for Everglades National Park was in Homestead, but the government housing for park employees was in nearby Florida City. Their GPS led them to their street, which dead-ended perpendicular to a canal. Their house was the last one on the right side. It looked sort of like a cabin, constructed of wooden logs with shake shingles.

"Wow," Emmet's dad said. "I had no idea."

"What?"

"If I'm not mistaken, the house is made out of cypress logs. And those are dwarf cypress trees in the backyard. I bet it's nice and cool inside."

When he opened the door, Apollo catapulted out of the truck. He climbed out slowly, his muscles stiff and achy. The little mutt went right to a bush by the front door, sniffed at it, declared it suitable, and then did what dogs do. The two of them stretched and tried to stifle yawns. Emmet jumped a little when the front door suddenly opened and a woman in a park-service uniform stepped out of their new house, followed by a boy about Emmet's age.

"You must be Dr. Doyle," she said, striding over to his dad and shaking his hand. "And you must be Emmet," she said, grinning at him. Her dark, curly hair was close-cropped, and she looked at them with the blackest eyes Emmet had ever seen. But they were friendly, kind of smiling in their own way, with little crinkles in the corners that curved upward when she grinned. Both she and the boy had deeply tanned olive-colored skin.

"I'm Dr. Geaux — Dr. Rosalita Geaux. This is my son, Calvin. I'm the lead research biologist and park superintendent here at the Everglades. I volunteered to make sure your house was ready before you got here. We like to make our new staff members feel welcome. Calvin, say hello."

"Hey," he said, raising his arm in a half wave, looking like he wanted to be there about as much as Emmet did, which was not much at all.

"Hello, Dr. Geaux. Hi, Calvin. This is my son, Emmet." Emmet was busy staring around the yard and the house, trying hard not to make snap judgments. His dad's voice brought him back to reality.

"Say hello, Emmet."

"Oh, hi," he said. Everyone stood there in silence for

a moment. They were saved by Apollo, who bounded up to Dr. Geaux and put his forepaws up on her waist.

"Well, well." She smiled, bending down to scratch Apollo behind the ears. For Apollo this was the equivalent of a person being given a million dollars out of the blue, and he licked Dr. Geaux's face with enthusiasm. She laughed and petted him some more.

"Look, Calvin, what a friendly little pooch!"

Calvin muttered something unintelligible, but Emmet liked Dr. Geaux a little more already. Anyone who lets a dog lick her face couldn't be all bad.

"Let me show you the house," Dr. Geaux said. She led them inside, and Emmet was glad to acknowledge that his dad was right — it was a lot cooler inside. The place was small but cozy, with the front door opening right into the living room. There was a hallway from there to the back of the house, with doors on each side of it leading to bedrooms and a large kitchen. The kitchen faced south. A big picture window over the sink and a skylight in the roof let in the sunlight, so the room was a lot brighter and more airy than the rest of the house.

"It was built in the thirties," Dr. Geaux said, "when most of the cypress trees in the Everglades were being cut down and used for building. The logs are almost two feet thick, which keeps the worst of the heat out. Plus, you could probably drop a bomb on it and it would still be standing. Back in 1992, Hurricane Andrew flattened almost everything in this entire area, but these old cypress houses lost maybe a few shingles and that was it. Solid as they come."

"It looks great," Dr. Doyle said. He always thought everything was "great," or "terrific," or "tremendous." The man was quiet and a little nerdy, but a relentless optimist. At least he used to be that way until Emmet's mom died. After that he didn't use words like that as often. It was kind of shocking to hear him use them again. But nice in a way, Emmet thought.

"Calvin," Dr. Geaux said. "Why don't you two check out the yard while I visit with Dr. Doyle for a spell." Dr. Geaux spoke with a slight accent, but her voice was kind and friendly. The boys went through the back door of the kitchen and into a good-sized yard. A wooden fence that matched the sun-faded color of the exterior of the house enclosed it. Apollo burst through the door and commenced an immediate inspection of the backyard, first stopping by one of the dwarf cypress trees. It appeared to meet his expectations and he moved on to the next. At least there was a little shade.

"What's his name?" Calvin asked.

"Apollo."

"Really?" he asked.

"Yeah. My mom used to read me all the stories from Greek mythology when I was a kid. Apollo was my favorite god," Emmet said.

"Is he a digger?" Calvin asked.

"A . . . what? I'm sorry?" Emmet asked.

"A digger. Would he try to dig his way out from under the fence?" Calvin wore a serious look on his face.

"I don't think so. He's a schnoodle, half poodle and half schnauzer, so he might dig after a gopher or a mole or something. Why?"

"There are gators in the canal. If he digs under the fence and leaves a big enough hole where he can get out — or where a gator could get in — well . . . he won't stand much chance against even a small one," Calvin said.

"Gators? You mean alligators? Right in the water behind my house?" Emmet asked.

"Yep. We are in a swamp, after all. That's where they tend to live. If they can get to it they'll eat most anything. My mom calls them 'opportunity' predators. They'll eat a cat or a dog same as they would a raccoon or a bird," Calvin said.

The news gave Emmet pause. Apollo was a great dog, but he also weighed about twenty pounds soaking wet. The trouble was, he thought he was a Rottweiler. Emmet shuddered at the thought of an alligator getting into the backyard.

"Just out of curiosity, how big do they get?" Emmet asked.

"Gators? Biggest one ever captured and recorded was just caught not long ago over near Winter Haven. Over twenty-eight feet long. Beat the old record by almost ten feet. It could have been two alligators taped together, it was so big. Most of the ones around here will get to be twelve to fourteen feet. You gotta watch out now, especially. It's spring, and when the babies hatch, the mama gators get real nasty," Calvin said.

"How'd you learn all this stuff?" Emmet asked, genuinely curious.

Calvin sighed and looked off over Emmet's shoulder at the sun-drenched sky. "My dad is . . . was a Seminole, and grew up here. He raised gators in the swamp. Ran a little business selling the teeth to tourists and the skins to companies making boots and purses and such. It was all completely legal. In fact, it's how he and my mom met. Before she was park superintendent she was a ranger here. She was on patrol in her boat and thought he was poaching. He'd found a baby gator tangled up in a net somebody left behind, and was trying to set it free. She thought he'd been using the net to catch 'em. Told him she was going to have to arrest him. He said, 'Not till after you have dinner with me.' Took her to his cabin to show her his permits, and explained what he was doing. They got married two years later."

"I can think of at least a hundred and sixty things I'd rather do than raise alligators. Does he still do it?" Emmet asked.

"No. He passed away six years ago," Calvin said.

"I'm sorry," Emmet said. He wanted to ask how, but he could tell Calvin didn't want to talk about it.

"My mom died a little over a year ago."

"I heard. From my mom," Calvin said.

"You figure that's why she brought you? Because we'd have something in common? Maybe be buds?" Emmet asked, a little annoyed at the way adults were always trying to manipulate things.

Calvin just shrugged, and Emmet felt bad immediately. It wasn't Calvin's fault.

"Sorry," Emmet said. "It's been a long trip and . . . sorry . . ." Calvin just shrugged again, and Emmet thought he was pretty low-key for someone who spent his whole life surrounded by alligators.

Their parents walked through the back door, interrupting the conversation.

"Well, you two look like you're getting to know each other," Dr. Geaux said.

"*Mom!*" Calvin said, his cheeks coloring. Emmet now officially felt sorry for him. He knew how he'd act if he'd been dragged along to meet some new kid, just because they had a dead parent in common.

"Calvin was just warning me about the alligators. Telling me to make sure Apollo leaves them alone and doesn't dig under the fence," Emmet said.

"Well, that's true, we wouldn't want anything to happen to this sweet puppy," Dr. Geaux said, bending down to scratch his ears again. It was abundantly clear. Apollo was in love.

"I'm guessing that's why we got the house with the fence," Dr. Doyle said.

"Yes, when you filled out your housing request it said you were dog owners. We try to accommodate the staff with outdoor pets. They get homes with fences around the yards. Alligators will come after house pets if they're hungry enough. And lately it seems like they're getting more and more aggressive," she said. "So don't take him anywhere outside the yard unless he's on a leash. Dogs don't realize the danger."

"Why?" Dr. Doyle said.

"Because it's their instinct . . ." she started to say.

"No, I mean why are the alligators becoming more aggressive?" Dr. Doyle said. Emmet recognized the look his dad was giving Dr. Geaux. His mom used to call it "scientist face." A problem had been presented. He needed to form a hypothesis.

"Dr. Doyle, did the NPS or anyone at your agency tell you specifically why you were assigned here?" she asked. *NPS* stood for *National Park Service*. Technically his dad worked for another department, the U.S. Fish and Wildlife Service, but he'd told Emmet he was being temporarily assigned to the NPS.

"Not really. My work orders just said 'special assignment,'" he said.

Dr. Geaux nodded. "It's true, the alligators here and around Homestead — and the entire southern end of the Everglades, for that matter — are moving in patterns we've not seen before." Just then, a bellowing sound came from the water beyond the fence, almost on cue. It sounded like a frog blowing on a giant kazoo.

"Bull," Calvin said. At first Emmet thought he was talking back to his mom.

"What?" Emmet asked.

"That was a bull gator, probably warning off another male." Calvin was the first twelve-year-old alligator expert Emmet had ever met.

"As I was saying," Dr. Geaux went on, "the population levels in the south end of the Glades are higher than they've been in nearly fifty years. But population counts deeper in the swamp are lower by almost the same percentage."

"Why do you think that is?" Dr. Doyle asked.

"I don't know," she said, running her hands through her hair. "But if I were to guess, I'd say something is driving them out. And we asked you here to help us find out what it is."

2

The Everglades

EMMET AND DR. DOYLE FOLLOWED DR. GEAUX AND Calvin back to Homestead, driving to the headquarters of Everglades National Park. It was a short trip and traffic was sparse. Emmet was amazed at the number of ponds and canals — water was everywhere. Birds and wildlife were all over the place. They passed a large group of alligators sunning themselves near one of the canals.

"Wow. That's quite a herd of killing machines," Emmet commented.

"Congregation," his dad said.

"Um. What?"

"A group of alligators is called a 'congregation.'"

"You mean like in a church?" Emmet asked.

Dr. Doyle chuckled. "Not exactly, although a church full of alligators would be something to see. No. It's just the name biologists call family groups of gators. Like a 'pride' of lions, or a 'rafter' of turkeys, or a 'troop' of baboons. Sometimes they're also called a 'float' or a 'bask,' but those terms are usually used for crocodiles."

"How do you know all this stuff?"

"I'm a biologist. I know *stuff.*"

"Aren't crocodiles and alligators the same?" Emmet asked.

"Similar, but no. In Florida, crocodiles are a much smaller population, and the species here can live in both freshwater and salt water. Alligators are fresh-water creatures only."

"Huh," Emmet said, looking out the window at the palm trees and hibiscus bushes and all the long-legged white birds standing around. It was a lot different from Montana. He missed the mountains. And he'd already learned more about alligators in an hour than he'd ever been interested in learning. Essentially, they were like grizzly bears in water. Grizzly bears with bigger mouths and more teeth.

"Dad," Emmet said. "I don't get something. If they've got an alligator problem, like Dr. Geaux said, why did they want you here? Your speciality is raptors." Raptors were birds of prey, a group that included eagles, hawks, and falcons. Dr. Doyle worked toward saving raptors from extinction. His methods for increasing the populations of various species of birds of prey were used in several states.

"I don't know. It might be a bird problem. Some raptors will feed on baby alligators. So an unusual invasion of birds of prey might make them migrate away from the danger. But that seems unlikely. It might have something to do with the similarities between birds and reptiles. As you know, they have a common evolutionary ancestor. . . ." He went on and Emmet breezed out. Dr. Doyle was in full-on bird-nerd mode. Emmet had perfected the art of half listening and nodding at the appropriate times.

". . . so I'm sure Dr. Geaux will fill us in when we get to the lab," his dad said about five minutes later.

"Right," he said as his dad wound down. Emmet heard only the words *birds, reptiles, common evolutionary ancestor,* and the name of a prehistoric creature he couldn't pronounce. Other than that, he didn't have a clue what his dad was talking about.

They followed Dr. Geaux's silver Buick past the main gate. A half mile farther down the road, another gate sat back off the street. She reached through her window and swiped a card through a reader box and the entrance swung open. They followed the car into the compound.

It was a good-sized building, with cedar siding and a covered porch along the front. They parked in a lot next to the building and joined Dr. Geaux, and a very bored-looking Calvin, waiting on the sidewalk. Per their instructions, Emmet held Apollo on a leash. The dog put his nose to the ground to smell the sidewalk, the grass, and Calvin's shoe, as if making sure nothing was past its expiration date.

"Oh dear, I forgot to tell you about the dog," Dr. Geaux said, with a grave look on her face.

"Huh?" Emmet asked.

She smiled. "I failed to inform you that as long as he's on a leash, Apollo is welcome in any of our buildings here at Everglades HQ."

Emmet let out a sigh of relief. He thought for a moment that he had violated a policy or something, and he didn't want to get his dad in trouble. Apollo was completely uninterested in the National Park Service HQ policy concerning dogs, as he was currently straining at his leash trying to reach a butterfly.

"Let's go," she said. They walked along the sidewalk to a building nestled in among a stand of palm trees. The building was aluminum sided, with a black-shingled roof. Dr. Geaux swiped a pass card through an electromagnetic lock on the door. It clicked open and they entered, and it felt like stepping into a refrigerator compared to the heat and humidity outside. The foyer was small, and before them stood a counter with a thick Plexiglas barrier reaching up to the ceiling, and a door to their right. Another swipe of the keycard and they were led to a large room with a cement floor. The room was lined with cages and long stainless-steel examination tables down its center. Most of the cages were filled with various animals: pelicans, raccoons, opossums, and several other birds and critters Emmet didn't recognize.

"This is our veterinary clinic," said Dr. Geaux. "We have rangers regularly patrolling the Glades, and any injured bird or animal we find is brought here to be treated."

"This is very impressive," Dr. Doyle said.

"Yes, well, we do what we can; as you know from working for a government agency, Dr. Doyle, budgets get cut and funding dries up. We have a lot of charitable contributions and private donors and fund-raisers, and we try the best we can to keep the Glades natural for everyone. But sometimes it feels like we're just holding our fingers in the floodgate," Dr. Geaux said. "More people are moving into Florida for the climate. There's pressure on the state to develop more and more of the land and distance themselves from the environmental lobbies. Some days . . ." She stopped to push her curly bangs back off of her forehead. "Well, let's just say there are days I feel my job is more about politics than science."

"That's why I stuck to fieldwork," Dr. Doyle said sympathetically. "I can't imagine the challenges you must face. I could never deal with it. But I bet you're very good at it."

Dr. Geaux smiled at Emmet's dad and said thank you. He didn't notice it, but her smile was different. Like she really appreciated what he said. The way she looked at him made Emmet a little uncomfortable. Although his dad was completely oblivious most of the time, Emmet wasn't. He thought maybe Dr. Geaux was crushing on his dad a little bit. The thought made him queasy, so he tried hard to think of something else. *Alligators! Alligators chasing me!* It only worked a little bit.

Dr. Geaux led them to the rear of the room. On the left-hand wall were four stainless-steel doors stacked two-on-two on top of each other. With her hand resting on the handle, she stopped.

"Emmet, you're about to see the reason that your father was ordered to the Everglades. It's something none of us have ever seen before. It may be what's causing the strange behavior of the alligators and other species in the park. We don't know what it is, but we can't let people get word of it. To be honest, at first I wasn't going to bring you along, but I know that with moving again, and all you've been through, it's only fair that you understand why we needed your dad. We've got a serious problem and he might be the best person to help us solve it. It's important work. But I understand what it means to be young and have to move to a new place. It's got to be hard. But you seem like a trustworthy young man, and I think it's only fair you are included. But you can't tell anyone.

"The press is already noticing something strange," Dr. Geaux went on. "With more alligators moving into the populated areas, they're becoming increasingly aggressive looking for food. You have to understand, people will panic over the slightest thing. And the media will fan the flames. The more attention and distractions we have, the harder it will be to get to the bottom of this. Does that make sense?"

Emmet liked that Dr. Geaux wasn't talking down to him like he was some kid. She was explaining, maybe lecturing a bit, but she was leaving the decision up to him.

"Yes, ma'am. I won't say anything," he said.

"That's good. You're on the team now," she said.

She opened the door and slid out a long panel. It was one of those refrigerated coolers like you see on police shows where the detectives go to the morgue and look at the dead body. There was something lying on the table covered in a white sheet. Dr. Geaux handed Dr. Doyle a pair of rubber gloves.

Removing the white sheet revealed a . . . something . . . sprawled on the slab. At first Emmet thought it was just an alligator. There was the familiar long tail, and the powerful snout with fearsome-looking teeth.

But it was lying on its back, and its feet were sticking up in the air and they looked . . . like bird feet.

"Whaaa?" Emmet said, unable to control himself, unconsciously taking a step back.

"Holy . . . !" Calvin said. "Mom, what is that thing?"

"A very good question, Calvin, a very good question, and I'm hoping Dr. Doyle will be able to help us figure it out," she said.

"I'm sorry, Dr. Geaux; I'm a field biologist, but my specialty is ornithology. Birds are my area, especially raptors," Dr. Doyle said. "I'm not sure why I'm here."

"I know your background, Dr. Doyle. In fact, it's why I requested you."

"I still don't understand," Dr. Doyle said. "Is this some previously undiscovered species of alligator or freshwater crocodile? It has been known to happen, even in places as well explored as the Everglades. In fact, an entirely new species of pigeon was just found —"

Dr. Geaux held up her hand. "No, Dr. Doyle. It's not a new species of reptile. But it is a new species. A new species of *what*, we aren't certain."

"But you must have run DNA tests?" Dr. Doyle asked.

Calvin and Emmet watched the two scientists talk, their heads going back and forth like they were sitting at a tennis match. Apollo quickly tired of all the talk and sprawled out, sleeping on the cool concrete floor at Emmet's feet.

"We did," Dr. Geaux said.

Dr. Doyle waited for her to speak, and when she didn't he said, "Well, what did they show?"

"We're not exactly sure. It has reptile DNA but it also has avian DNA," she said.

The look of disbelief on his dad's face made Emmet think he'd been hit by a two-by-four.

"That's impossible. There must be some mistake!" he insisted.

Dr. Geaux shook her head. "We ran them twice. Different tissue samples, same result."

Dr. Doyle looked down at the creature lying on the slab and studied it, his eyes roaming over the carcass from head to tail. Emmet saw that he was in full-on "scientist face" mode. Emmet studied the corpse of the . . . bird-a-gator . . . as well. He couldn't help but imagine it springing back to life and attacking them with flashing claws and snapping jaws. Looking at it made him think of the worst kind of monster in any horror movie he'd ever seen. It gave him the willies.

"Then what in the heck is this thing?" Dr. Doyle asked.

"That's a very good question," Dr. Geaux said. "Welcome to the team."

She looked at Emmet and Calvin. "Calvin, why don't you take Emmet down to the dock, maybe take him and Apollo for a spin in our airboat. Dr. Doyle and I need to talk."

3

FROM A COMPOUND HIDDEN NEAR THE NORTHERN EDGE of the Everglades, a man sat at a bank of computer screens and monitors. The building was prefabricated and set deep into the swampy soil. Construction crews he flew in illegally from South America brought the structure here in pieces. Once it was assembled he sent them back home. And from his secret hideaway, his work began in earnest. It was from here he set out to stop the destruction of the Everglades.

No one would ever find this place. The building was dark concrete and the outside walls and roof were covered with native vegetation. The roof was too thick for heat to escape, and the power came from a place no one would ever suspect, more than a mile away. He used specially designed waterproof cables to carry the electricity beneath the swamp to his compound. Even if someone were to uncover the deeply buried cables, it would still be a Herculean task to trace them this far. At night, two wind turbines emerged from specially built shafts at the rear of the building and wind energy generated power to backup batteries that could keep the compound running for nearly three days, should the generators go down. Long enough for him to fix the problem or evacuate to a backup location much like this one but in a place just as hard to find.

The building held three rooms. A computer room and monitoring station where he sat now, a small sleeping room with a kitchenette, and his lab. The lab was the largest section of his base, where his instruments and specimens were kept. It was here he did his work. His divine mission. Making Mother Nature whole again. Saving the Everglades from not only the ravages of man but also the invasive species destroying the ecosystem.

On the monitor in front of him, he watched a split screen. One image showed Dr. Geaux and the new scientist; she called him Dr. Doyle. He ran an Internet search about this new man, sending pages and links to his tablet to be read later. Know your enemy. They were examining the carcass of one of his creations. It was an unfortunate accident to lose one of his pets. He was desperate to figure out what had happened and it was just bad luck that a park ranger stumbled upon the corpse before he could retrieve it.

Now he watched Geaux and Doyle as they examined the animal he created. He slid a knob on the panel in front of him and brought up the audio. They were discussing x-rays and Dr. Doyle was studying the skeletal structure. "Fascinating," he heard Dr. Doyle say.

He watched as they worked and exchanged ideas, laughing at some of their theories and suggestions. But he could not afford to be smug. He was not above realizing there were other brilliant minds out there. If someone put the pieces together, his entire plan could collapse. Luckily, unknown to Dr. Geaux, he had access to Everglades Park HQ. If she knew who he really was, she would be shocked. And that access allowed him to place hidden video cameras and recording devices all over the NPS headquarters. It was one way to stay ahead of them. Leaning back in his chair, he massaged his neck muscles. He slept only four hours a night. His mission demanded it. He could not allow human weakness to interrupt his work. Another image on the monitor caught his eye. The two boys arrived at the facility with the doctors. Outside the NPS lab, they walked along the wooden dock to where the NPS airboats were parked. The Doyle boy led a small black dog on a leash.

He watched as they reached a smaller airboat at the very end of the line. He knew this was Dr. Geaux's personal craft. After monitoring her activities for months, it was clear she was a total by-the-books superintendent, and would never allow the boy to use an NPS boat. They boarded, and her son expertly started it up and it backed away from the dock.

This was interesting. He grabbed the keys to his own airboat, also hidden from sight next to the compound. Dr. Geaux gave permission for the boys to head out on their boat and explore the swamp. It would be dark soon. They would be alone.

Perhaps this interruption to his plan could be rectified.

4

DR. DOYLE WAS CONCERNED ABOUT THE BOYS GOING ON the boat alone, but Dr. Geaux reassured him.

"Calvin has been piloting an airboat since he was six years old. He's probably the best Everglades guide in the state under eighteen," she said.

Emmet could tell his dad was about to say no, when he gave him a pleading look. "*Dad!*" he said. "It'll be fine. We won't be gone long; I'm sure Calvin knows how to drive a boat."

"Pilot," Calvin said.

"Huh, what?" Emmet asked.

"You pilot a boat. Not drive it."

"Oh. Dad. Please, may I go on a boat-*piloting* trip with

Calvin? Then you can get all scientisty and stuff with Dr. Geaux," Emmet begged.

His dad could be so thick sometimes. This was one of those times.

"I don't suppose it could hurt," Dr. Doyle said, looking at his watch. "It's going to be dark soon, though, so be sure to be —"

"Great. Have fun with your . . . whatever it is you're going to do. C'mon, Apollo. Boat ride."

With Apollo in tow, they exited the lab and walked along a gravel-covered path that led deeper into the trees. About a half mile behind the compound they came to a dock with several NPS boats secured to it. At the end was a smaller, sleeker airboat. There were two seats in the front and another behind those, where the pilot sat and operated the motor and tiller. Behind the pilot's seat was a large fan, enclosed in a metal frame. Emmet had seen airboats on television and knew the fan would spin and the air it pushed would propel the boat, skimming across the water. Usually at a high rate of speed. Painted on the side was DRAGONFLY 1. And Calvin was surprised by how much it did remind him of a dragonfly.

"I don't know a thing about boats, obviously. But that thing looks incredibly fast," Emmet said.

"It is," Calvin said.

"Look, I know your mom suggested this. If you don't want to go out, it's cool," Emmet said.

"No, it's fine. I'll take any excuse to go out on the water."

"Will Apollo be okay or should I leave him with my dad?"

"He can come. Most dogs seem to enjoy it," Calvin said.

The boat was secured in its slip, with two lines around wooden posts fore and aft. When they stepped on board it bobbed gently in the water. Emmet was amazed at how clean and spotless the inside of the boat was. Everything fit neatly in a holder, nook, or cranny.

On the dashboard next to the pilot's seat was a clear plastic sheath with a card inside it. Calvin removed it, and the felt marker attached to it with a clip. He wrote some information down on the card.

"What are you writing?" Emmet asked.

"It's our 'float plan.' I'm recording the date, time, and number of passengers, and where I intend to go and when I expect to be back. If we have engine trouble or some kind of emergency where we have to leave the boat, it will give a rescue party the information they need to help coordinate a search," Calvin explained.

"Um. Excuse me for asking, but do you have engine trouble and have to leave the boat very often?" Emmet asked.

Calvin scowled. "Never. It's just a precaution. Something my dad taught me. Cast off fore and aft, if you don't mind." Emmet wasn't sure what that meant exactly, but he'd seen some TV shows and movies where "cast off" meant to take the ropes off the pilings attached to the dock. Calvin started up the engine and it growled to life. When the radio came on, he spoke into the microphone.

"NPS base, this is *Dragonfly One*, come in," he said.

"*Dragonfly One*, I read you five by five. That you, Calvin?" a voice on the other end answered.

"Ten-four, Manny, how you doing?" Calvin said.

"I'm great, my man. You going out?" Manny said. Emmet thought he sounded like one of the happiest people he'd ever heard.

"Roger that, Manny. A quick trip. Just out to Hawkins Flats and back. Anything I should know? How's the weather?"

"No worries, Little Papi, we might get some showers tonight, but it looks clear for now. I don't have anybody showing on the board in that area, but you know that don't mean anything. Not everybody is as good about filing their float plans as you are," Manny said.

"I learned from the best," Calvin said.

"Roger that, Little Papi. Check in when you get back. You got the battery on the GPS charged?"

"Ten-four, Manny, you do know who you're talking to, right?"

"Had to ask, my man. You be careful," Manny answered back.

"Ten-four, *Dragonfly One* out," Calvin said.

Calvin slipped the microphone into its slot on the side of the radio console.

"Ready?" he asked.

"As I'll ever be," Emmet answered.

Emmet sat in one of the front seats and strapped in. Apollo jumped into the seat next to him and he wrapped the leash tightly around his wrist. Calvin reversed throttle and the boat backed away from the dock. When it was clear, he pushed the tiller to the left and Emmet felt a little jolt as the craft took a small leap forward.

Working their way out toward open water, Calvin kept the airboat at a slow cruising speed, the engine rumbling as they left the NPS compound behind. When they were out of the "No Wake Zone," Calvin hit the main power for the fan and opened the throttle. Emmet was catapulted back into his seat.

The huge fan started spinning and the boat skimmed across the water like the dragonfly it was named for. Emmet was shocked at the speed, and the loudness of the fan. Apollo sat up in the seat and put his face into the wind, the smells of the swamp assaulting his nose, and he appeared to enjoy every second of it. There was much more open water than Emmet expected. He'd pictured a swamp as a place overgrown with strange plants, big dark trees covered in moss blocking out the sunlight, and full of scary animals. Well, with that "whatever the heck it was" lying in the lab, they apparently had the scary-animals part covered.

But as they skimmed across the water, the wind whipping through his hair, Emmet was amazed at how it continued to surprise him. There were plenty of trees — cypress and mangrove and other kinds he didn't know yet. And every species of bird he could imagine: herons, egrets, and even an osprey soaring high on the wind currents. He thought it was the biggest bird he might ever have seen. And that included all the bald eagles he'd seen in Montana.

Expectations. His mom always told him to keep an open mind. If he did so, "people and places would surprise you," she would say. And he was surprised. His mom and dad loved the outdoors and passed the love on to him. He couldn't say the Everglades were more beautiful than Montana, just beautiful in a different way.

They approached a spot where a small island rose up out of the water. Calvin cut the engine and the boat slowed. Emmet couldn't help but think of the little lump ahead of them as an oasis, only instead of in the desert, it was in the middle of a swamp. The boat floated until it bumped against the sandy shore.

Calvin undid his harness and passed between Emmet and Apollo, tying the line securely to the root of a mangrove tree. He stepped out of the boat over the bow, onto the shore.

"So what do you think?" he asked Emmet.

"It's not what I expected. But it's pretty awesome in its own way," Emmet said. "Um. What are we doing now?"

"Thought you might want to take a stroll around this little island. See some of the birds and wildlife," Calvin said.

"Stroll. Okay. Like, just take a walk around?" Emmet asked.

"Yep."

Emmet sat in the boat. Apollo was poised, trembling, on the edge of his seat, his nose working the air. He was desperate to jump out and follow Calvin, and give the island a good smelling-over. Emmet looked to the left and right and then over Calvin's shoulder as if he were studying the interior of the island and counting the mangrove and cypress trees.

"Is there a problem?" Calvin asked.

"Oh, no. No problem. Well. Yes. No. I don't . . . maybe," Emmet stammered.

"And that would be . . ." Calvin waited.

"Alligators. Just wondering if there might be alligators on this island, is all. Or actually . . . if there are any nearby right now. In the immediate vicinity. Of us?"

Calvin kept a straight face. He put his hand over his eyes, as if shading them from the sun, and studied the horizon in both directions. Squatting, he picked up a handful of sand, smelling it first, and then letting it dribble to the ground. A small clump of grass poked out of the ground by Calvin's foot and he pulled out a few strands, threw them up in the air, and watched the direction they were carried by the breeze.

Emmet was dying of curiosity.

"Is that some kind of way to test if alligators are around?" Emmet asked.

Calvin nodded yes. Then smiled. "No. I have no idea if there are alligators close by. This is the Everglades. They're all over the place. We'll be fine. We just make noise when we walk, it will scare them away. Come on, you'll like it."

"Oh, so funny," Emmet said. *Guy thinks he's a comedian,* he thought.

Calvin stood and started walking along the shore. "Did you know gators can hear, see, and smell way better than humans? A mama gator can hear her babies squeaking inside the eggs when they're ready to hatch. They'll either hear us coming and leave, or see us before we see them. And they stay close to the water. So don't worry."

41

Emmet stood in the boat and tightened his grip on Apollo's leash. They stepped over the bow and onto the shore. Emmet grimaced as he followed Calvin.

"Smart aleck," he muttered.

"Seriously. We'll be fine," Calvin said. "You'll see. Unless we stumble across a nest and the cow is around. That usually doesn't end well."

"Wait. What?" Emmet said, his stomach lurching.

But Calvin disappeared through a tangle of mangroves. Apollo strained at the leash to follow after him. Emmet gave his traitorous dog a glare.

"Wise guy," he said. And the two of them followed Calvin into the trees.

5

LIKE THE COMPOUND DEEP IN THE SWAMP, THE MAN'S airboat was also specially constructed. It was powered by an electrical motor, with an alternate gasoline one, and the composite plastics and fiberglass of its hull made it both lighter and nearly indestructible. The newly designed motor could run for up to eight hours on battery power, and because of the decreased weight from its hull it was faster and more maneuverable than any boat operating in the swamp. The electric motor was quiet, allowing him to navigate in near silence. In an emergency he could switch to the gas-powered motor and speed away from any unexpected danger.

His compound, the boat, all of it was part of his carefully orchestrated plan. He was not a fool. There would be those opposed to his method. Geniuses and revolutionary thinkers like him were always misunderstood and cast as villains, at least at first. Undoubtedly there would be those who would try to stop him if his plans were revealed. Dr. Geaux and the bureaucracy she worked for would look down on his solutions, of that he was sure.

Let her. Let them. He did not care. He would not stop.

His beloved Everglades would be saved. He was at a critical point now and that was why losing his specimen was so distressing. It came at the worst possible time. Then it became a bigger problem when the corpse was discovered and delivered to Dr. Geaux. Somehow he must reclaim the body and find a way to regain control of the situation. Something to draw Dr. Geaux's, and her new cohort, Dr. Doyle's, attention away from the project. It might give him the window he needed to recover it.

His boat flew across the water. On the screen before him the small blip showed the location of the craft the two boys were in. It stopped at the small island that stood at the mouth of Anhinga Creek, where it emptied into the Taylor Slough. It was spring, and the water was still high in the slough, so he should have no trouble piloting his boat. Come summer, the water often dried up, making it impossible to travel even by airboat. The boys were probably exploring the island, as he had done when he was their age. It was a risk moving about in the daylight like this. But it was one he must take. His boat traveled the distance to the island in a few minutes.

The two long wire cages at the bow of his twenty-foot craft were not empty. Inside were two of the Pterogators created in his lab. They were among the very first to hatch after he perfected the gene-splicing and DNA-sequencing techniques that led to their creation. It was an amazing accomplishment, turning back the evolutionary clock. Someday he would likely be awarded a Nobel Prize.

But not quite yet. Now there was more work to do. Slowing the boat as the island came into sight, he approached from the west. Through his binoculars he studied the airboat and the shore. There was no sign of the boys, or the dog. They were likely on the far side now. Still, he needed to work quickly, and he expertly maneuvered his boat next to the *Dragonfly 1*. They collided with a gentle *thump*. Quickly he stepped onto the smaller boat. Kneeling behind the pilot's chair, he lifted the access panel to the engine compartment. After disconnecting the spark-plug wire and removing the fuel line, he shut it and unplugged the microphone from the radio, tossing it onto his boat. The *Dragonfly 1* was now powerless and couldn't call for help. He didn't know if the boys carried cell phones, but there was nothing he could do about that.

Returning to his boat, he pushed a button on his tablet computer and the side gates on the cages opened. His two lovelies were released. They crawled out of the cages and onto the sandy shore of the island. He watched them move with great satisfaction. His scientific training had taught him not to give animals human characteristics, but he could not resist and had named them Hammer and Nails.

They were specially bred to hunt the large snakes devastating the Everglades. He was reasonably sure they wouldn't harm the boys. But it would give them a good scare. And if he was lucky, once she learned of it, Dr. Geaux would close down the park, giving him free reign to save it. To be the catalyst for the change needed to save the environment.

Catalyst.

He liked the sound of that.

6

"DID YOU HEAR THAT?" EMMET ASKED.

"What?" Calvin answered.

"It sounded like a splash. From that way." He pointed toward the eastern point of the island. "Or maybe that way."

"When you're around water you tend to hear splashes," Calvin said patiently.

"Ha. Very funny. This alligator thing is freaking me out."

"Look, you can't be like that. Ninety-nine percent of the time, an alligator is not going to view you as either a threat or a meal. If you don't do something stupid, like get between a mother and her babies, or corner it, or poke it with a stick, or try to play cards with it, they're just going to slip into the water and swim away. Gators are a fact of life down here. Besides, didn't you have grizzly bears in Montana?" Calvin asked.

"Yes. But you didn't tend to see grizzly bears sunning themselves by the side of the road. And they have fewer teeth. And what is this 'ninety-nine percent' stuff? What about the other one percent?" Emmet said.

"The other one percent of the time you're gator bait," Calvin said matter-of-factly. They reached the other side of the small island. Nearby, a nesting cormorant took flight. The flap of wings and resulting squawk made Emmet jump. He took a deep breath to calm his nerves. Apollo jerked the leash and barked. His dislike of birds was intense.

"Are you always such a comedian?" Emmet asked.

Calvin shrugged. He watched the cormorant circle the sky above them.

"Come on," he said. "We're making mama bird nervous."

"She's not alone," Emmet said.

They walked along the shore, Apollo in strange-odor sensory overload, darting back and forth, smelling everything and nothing all at once. Now they stood on the north end. The whole island was maybe seventy-five yards wide and one hundred yards long. Calvin recited the names of trees, plants, and birds. Emmet couldn't remember ever seeing so many different species of birds in one place. His dad, the bird nerd, was probably going to pass out. There were anhinga, egrets, herons, and ospreys. It was enough to drive poor Apollo to apoplexy.

Emmet couldn't say exactly when his feeling of being watched started. It may have been when Apollo stopped and alerted, growling and nearly pulling free from the leash. The dog peered into the trees massed on the center of the island — small, excited yips escaping his throat. Apollo was straining so hard at his leash, Emmet was forced to lean back to keep from stumbling.

Or it might have been the feeling, a tickle along the back of his neck. Calvin didn't seem to notice, and for a brief moment Emmet saw how different Calvin was out in the swamp compared to how he appeared earlier in the day. There was a peaceful look on his face. He clearly felt at home here.

Emmet heard a noise, a large rustling sound in the interior of the island, high in the trees.

"Did you hear that?" Emmet asked.

"What?"

"That noise, like something in the treetops," Emmet said.

"I didn't hear anything. Relax. It's probably just a bird."

Apollo jerked at the leash and whined now, ready to hurl all twenty pounds of his righteous fury upon whatever was stalking them. Emmet looked, and this time there was more and louder rustling, and he saw branches and leaves moving.

"There's something there. And it's coming this way. Seriously, dude," Emmet said.

Calvin looked. His eyes narrowed and he studied the copse of trees, his head cocked, listening. The wind was in their faces, and Apollo was sniffing like he was a contestant in the world's-most-sniffingest-dog contest.

"Probably just a bird," Calvin said.

"I don't think so," Emmet said.

"Based on what?" Calvin asked. The words were hardly out of his mouth before they heard a strange cross between a grunt and what sounded like an extremely angry lion.

"Was that a gator?" Emmet asked, reaching down and scooping Apollo up in his arms. The dog struggled to get free. Emmet wrapped the leash around his wrist a few more times and told Apollo to settle down. With limited effect.

"I . . . don't know. It sort of sounded like one, but not exactly. . . ." Calvin muttered, still studying the trees. The branches of one of the taller trees, maybe fifty yards away from where they stood, clearly shook this time. The weird noise sounded again. Apollo couldn't control himself, and let loose with a full-on onslaught of barks, still wiggling and trying to free himself from Emmet's grasp.

Curiously, the branches stopped moving, and the strange call was silenced by Apollo's anger. This only made Emmet feel more uneasy, because the feeling of being watched was impossible to ignore. Now he felt a little bit like a fly trying to get free from a spider's web, but the spider was getting closer.

"I think we should go back to the boat," Calvin said quietly.

"I'm not going back through there!" Emmet said.

"No. We'll walk along the shore, circle around that way," Calvin said. He moved to the water line, keeping his eyes on the trees, which only made Emmet feel more creeped out.

"What do you think it is?"

Calvin shrugged, but was picking up his pace. Emmet was still carrying Apollo, and struggled to keep up while contending with his squirming dog.

"I'm pretty sure it was a gator," Calvin said. "Might be a nest in there. Mama calling to the babies, probably, except . . ."

"Except what? And wait a minute! We just walked through there a little while ago. Did we go past a nest?" Emmet was freaking out a little bit.

"We could have . . . it's just . . . it's a little early in the spring for eggs to hatch," Calvin said.

"But baby alligators . . . don't they just run to the water after they hatch, like sea turtles or something?" Emmet asked.

"No. Mama gators take care of their young. They stay near the nest until they're big enough to survive on their own. If there's trouble or a predator, she'll call them and they will swim or crawl into her mouth for protection," Calvin replied.

"You're kidding!"

"Not about gators," Calvin said.

"No, I suppose not. But what do you think that was in the trees? They can't climb, can they?"

"No, they can't climb. I'm not sure what it is. It might be a panther," Calvin said. The boat lay up ahead, bobbing gently in the water. It was a welcome sight to Emmet. Then he remembered that Calvin just said *panther*.

"A panther? What kind of island did you bring me to?"

"I'm just guessing. It might have been on the southern end and heard us, or smelled us when we walked through. It's probably just curious. Still, they're critically endangered down here, so we should leave it alone," Calvin said.

"Gladly," Emmet said.

Apollo was still a little furry ball of rage, barking and growling while he struggled mightily to be free. When they stepped into the boat, Emmet set the dog in the seat and hooked his leash to it. Apollo stood up, his body rigid, growling toward the trees in the center of the island. Calvin untied the line from the mangrove root and took his seat at the tiller. He pushed the ignition button and there was a whirring, then a clicking sound.

"Dang," Calvin said.

"What?" Emmet said.

"I don't know . . . yet." He tried the button again and was rewarded with another whir and more clicks. Calvin knelt behind his seat and pulled up a panel on the deck over the engine compartment. He jiggled some wires and turned a couple of knobs and tried the ignition again. Nothing.

"I'm going to have to radio base and arrange for a tow. We . . ." He stopped speaking and Emmet looked back at him.

"What?" Emmet asked.

"The microphone is gone," Calvin said.

"How?"

"I don't know. It was there when we left," Calvin said.

Right then, Apollo went berserk. He barked crazily and jumped off the seat, running the length of his leash until it jerked him to a stop. Calvin and Emmet looked up to find what occupied his attention. They both immediately wished they hadn't.

Crawling slowly out of the trees and heading toward

the boat across the sand came not one but two creatures just like the one that lay in Dr. Geaux's lab. As terrifying as the dead one was, alive they were even more frightening. One of them opened its mouth and bugled with the awful croaking roar they heard earlier.

Both of them were headed straight for the boat.

7

OFFSHORE, THE MAN WATCHED THE EVENTS ON THE island through his binoculars. His boat was camouflaged, and he positioned it behind a small patch of saw grass clinging to a mound of soil sticking up out of the water. His pets were behaving strangely. It wasn't like them to take an interest in anything that wasn't a snake.

Still, he was reluctant to act. He wouldn't allow the boys to come to any real harm. But carefully managed, this situation could work to his advantage. If Dr. Geaux believed that more of his creations roamed the swamp, she would proceed with caution. Perhaps even taking the unprecedented step of closing the Everglades to all visitors. Which was his ultimate goal. He intended to restore the ecosystem there to its original pristine state. Nothing less would satisfy him.

He watched as the hybrids crept across the sand toward the airboat. Calvin was a cool customer, not panicking like most boys his age would. They were out of earshot, but he could see them talking and hear the muffled sounds of their raised voices.

Now he studied his creations' behavior as they approached the boat. Seeing them act this way was mildly alarming. His intention was for the boys to be frightened off by the rustling in the bushes and the unique sound of their fearsome call. For some reason, Hammer and Nails left the cover of the trees, now acting as if they would attack the boys. He decided to let them get a little closer before activating their beacons. But hopefully this field observation would give him some insight into why one of his specimens now lay dead in Dr. Geaux's lab.

Could it be the constant and infernal barking of the dog? Did the noise awaken some primitive avian or reptilian response, which caused their genetically altered brains to focus on the canine? Might that be what happened to the earlier specimen Dr. Geaux found? His data said it was highly unlikely. Carefully controlled tests showed that the creatures fixated solely on pythons and boa constrictors. Even when offered an easier opportunity for prey, they were fed only snake meat from the time they hatched. The avian strain of the great gray owl, a bird of prey known for its love of snakes, had overridden the alligators' desire to eat the easiest thing to catch. Given that raptors like the owl could be trained, he was certain he had created the perfect snake-killing machine.

So why were they reacting this way?

Hammer and Nails were now almost at the boat. One of the boys was using the boat hook to pole the boat backward into the water. Perhaps it was a mistake to disable their boat and take the microphone. All he wanted to do was put a healthy scare into them.

The dog was nearly crazed now and barking so much its voice was growing hoarse. The creatures were at the water's edge and seemed fixated on the black-haired mutt. It was time to reassert control of the situation.

He pressed the button on the console that activated their homing collars. Hammer and Nails stopped and looked in the direction of his boat. They backed up on the sandy shore and held still, appearing confused. Their heads swiveled back and forth, looking at the nearby boat and toward his position.

Frantically, his fingers flew over the tablet, adjusting the beacon's intensity and frequency. The two Pterogators still did not respond. To his horror, they ignored his signal and turned their attention back to the boys, the dog, and their stranded boat.

8

"WHAT DO WE DO?" EMMET SAID, HIS VOICE RISING in pitch.

"Remain calm," Calvin said, his hands still buried in the engine hatch.

"REMAIN CALM? Have you looked around? There's a couple of . . . of . . . of . . . *velociraptors* about to climb in the boat with us!" Emmet yelled.

"Use the boat hook, don't let them get aboard." Calvin barely raised his voice while he worked on the engine. "Do you have a cell phone?"

"NO!" Emmet said. "Do you?"

"Nope. Don't really like 'em," Calvin said quietly. His focus and calmness were starting to irk Emmet. Emmet picked up the boat hook, which was about the size of a broomstick. He groaned. They were probably the only two kids in America who didn't have cell phones.

"This seems pretty inadequate given our current situation," Emmet said, hefting the boat hook. "This airboat doesn't come with a rocket launcher, does it?" With the noise Apollo was making, he nearly had to shout. He'd given up trying to quiet the dog.

Emmet held the boat hook out in front of him and stepped slowly toward the bow. They were floating about ten yards off shore and the scare-a-gators were about to enter the water.

Then the creatures stopped moving and looked off into the distance, like a dog might upon hearing a whistle outside of human hearing range. Emmet wasn't sure at first, but he thought something was blinking by their throats. The red light flashed again and this time he saw it clearly. They were wearing collars. Whatever was happening momentarily distracted them, and Emmet took the opportunity to poke the boat hook into the water. He pushed back against the bottom and shoved them a few feet farther away.

The creatures appeared confused. When the red light started blinking more rapidly, Emmet pushed harder, until he could no longer reach the bottom.

"They're wearing some kind of collar!" Emmet said. Apollo appeared to have barked himself out, and now stood trembling on the seat, growling and whining.

His body was rigid and the hair along his back stood straight up.

"What?" Calvin said, looking up from the hatch.

"They've got collars . . . for tracking, or so they don't bark or something," Emmet said, gripping the boat hook tighter.

"Huh," Calvin said.

"Huh? Huh?" Emmet said. "That's it?"

"I've almost got the engine fixed," Calvin said.

The creatures turned their focus back to the boat. They were almost in the water now, their tails swishing.

"You better hurry —" Emmet said. His words were cut off and he flinched as Calvin flew past him, holding two emergency flares. He struck the heads of the flares against each other and they burst into flame, a bright red light dancing at the end of each one. Calvin jumped off the front of the boat into the waist-deep water, waving the flares at the two critters and shouting.

His charge caught them off guard, and they backed away onto the shore. Calvin splashed through the water, kicking and screaming, waving the flares. When they backed up far enough, he tossed the flares up on the shore, each one landing in the sand in front of the creatures. The hissing flames drove them back farther.

Calvin waded back to the boat and hopped in.

"Keep an eye on them," he said. He hurried back to the engine hatch and knelt beside it again. His hands disappeared inside. A few seconds later he stood and hit the ignition switch, and the engine roared to life.

"Buckle up!" he shouted.

Stunned, Emmet fastened himself into his seat and grabbed ahold of Apollo's leash. Calvin turned the boat and they roared away, leaving the two creatures on the shore behind them.

9

"**W**HAT?!" EMMET SAID, UNABLE TO KEEP THE SUR-prise and shock out of his voice. "Are you serious? I am not going back to that island! In fact, Dad, pack a bag. We're leaving Florida immediately." Emmet paced nervously in the small office outside the lab. Dr. Geaux used it when she had to work in this building. Her official office was in the park headquarters building. The shelves were lined with books and photos. Several of the pictures showed Calvin at various stages of growth, his dark curly hair in evidence through each one. Some of the photographs showed Dr. Geaux, Calvin, and a man doing different things: relaxing on the beach, driving the airboat, fishing, sitting by a Christmas tree. The man was a bigger version of Calvin. Emmet decided he must have been his father.

Dr. Geaux remained calm, running her hands through her curly, short black hair. Emmet was anything but. When they'd returned to the compound, they raced from the dock back to the lab and found both of their parents still working on the specimen. When they explained what happened, Dr. Geaux went into action, summoning two park rangers she trusted. Their last names were Clark and Marcus. Now she wanted them all to go back to "the scene."

Emmet couldn't believe it.

"Uh. No, thank you, I'll pass! We were almost devoured by . . . by . . . those owl-a-gators! I'm not going back out there! No possible way!" Emmet was adamant.

"Owl-a-gators?" Dr. Doyle asked, genuinely confused.

"Yeah . . . they've got those weird necks and eyes and their faces sort of look like owls. Don't interrupt me mid-rant! What the heck kind of place is this? I want to go back to Montana right now!" Emmet stalked back and forth across the floor of the lab, trying and failing to make himself stop shaking. Calvin, after being given the mom inspection and found uninjured, was leaning serenely against the wall with his arms crossed, as if he had just awoken from a nap.

Emmet stopped pacing and looked at Calvin.

"How did you fix the boat, anyway?" he asked.

Calvin shrugged. "The fuel line was removed. It's fairly easy to do if you know your way around an engine. Luckily, because airboats sometimes get dirt in the fuel line, we keep a spare duct-taped to the engine hatch. It just snaps in place with a clip at each end. Whoever removed it didn't take the spare."

"And you're sure it was taken? It didn't just come loose?" Dr. Geaux asked.

Calvin looked at his mother and blinked a few times before answering. Emmet wondered if this was the Calvin equivalent of a tantrum.

"Yes, Mom. Somebody took it. It would need to 'come loose' on both ends. And besides, whoever did it also took the radio mic to make sure we couldn't call for help." Calvin looked down at the floor then, as if to say that this part of the conversation was over.

"All right," Dr. Geaux said. "I guess you boys can stay here. Rangers Clark, Marcus, and I will take two boats out to the island. Dr. Doyle, I would appreciate your having a look as well, but I understand if you want to remain behind with Emmet."

Dr. Doyle looked at her and then Emmet. He was about to speak, but Emmet beat him to it.

"Wait a minute! You're not going out there and leaving us here alone! Not with those things on the loose," Emmet said.

"Emmet . . ." Dr. Doyle started to speak, but Dr. Geaux cut him off.

"No, it's okay, Benton. I understand Emmet's point. It's not been the best introduction to Florida. But Calvin understands I have a responsibility as park director to investigate." She waited to see what the two of them would say next.

"Oh, no you don't. I'm not falling into the 'I have a responsibility' trap. I have a responsibility, too! To myself! To not get eaten! I'm not going anywhere. Dad, if you need to go, fine. But I'm staying here until you get back. Right here. In this office. With the door closed. And locked. I'm pretty sure those . . . croco-whatevers . . . can't pick locks. Although I wouldn't be surprised if they could."

"I'll stay with you, Emmet," Dr. Doyle said quietly. "I know you're scared. It'll be okay."

Dr. Geaux stood up and looked at Calvin. "Do you want to stay? You know I have to investigate, right?"

"I don't mind going out with you, Mom. But you should make sure the rangers take rifles. Those things didn't act like regular gators. . . . Well . . . maybe gators on steroids," Calvin said.

"Benton," Dr. Geaux said. "Would you and Emmet mind remaining here until we return? It's almost dark, and we won't be out long. But if there's anything to see, I don't want to leave it until tomorrow. If we find . . .

something, I'd like you to be here in case we need to examine . . . in case we need you."

"Certainly. We'll wait until you return, Rosalita. Be careful," Dr. Doyle said. She nodded, and Emmet and Dr. Doyle watched as they left the building.

"Geez," Emmet said.

"Are you sure you're okay?" his dad asked.

"Physically. But I'm going to have nightmares for the rest of my life. I mean it. For. Ever. But that Calvin kid. He's . . . he's . . ." Emmet couldn't think of the right words. He sat down in a chair next to Dr. Geaux's desk and Apollo hopped up into his lap, licking his face.

"He's what?" Dr. Doyle prodded Emmet.

"Not normal!" Emmet was freaking out. His dad was as cool as the other side of the pillow. "Those things were going to eat us and he's all 'Hold them off with the boat hook.' And I'm all 'A boat hook! We need a machine gun!' And he's all 'Let me fix my engine with some duct tape and spit.' Holy moly! We could have been killed!" Emmet sat, stiff as a board, on the chair.

"Sounds like he's at home in the swamp," Dr. Doyle said, trying to settle Emmet down.

"I'll say. We heard a noise up in the trees and saw the leaves and branches moving, and then this weird growling, crying sound. Apollo starts going nuts, and Calvin says, 'Oh, it's probably just a panther.' Like he might have been describing a kitten. A panther! Who does that? And I knew Florida has alligators — I mean I watch TV. But you never said anything about panthers or those, those . . ."

"What did you call them, again?" Dr. Doyle asked.

"I . . . I don't remember. It's weird. Their faces, or snouts or whatever, look like birds somehow. It's . . ." Emmet went on, "Why didn't you tell me about those? I've never heard of them before!"

"That's because they've never existed before. At least, not in this form, and not for a very long time," Dr. Doyle said, looking out the window of Dr. Geaux's office.

"Wait. What? Slow down, Dad. I'm not a scientist. What did you just say?" Emmet's nerves were still jangled, although Apollo, in his dog's mind having vanquished the creatures in battle, curled up in his lap and went to sleep.

"Dr. Geaux and I have come up with a preliminary theory. We don't think these creatures are naturally evolved," Dr. Doyle said.

"Huh? What do you mean, 'naturally evolved'? My brain hurts. I just about got eaten by a couple of dino-gators or . . . whatever," Emmet complained.

"We don't think these creatures are . . . real manifestations of natural selection or even crossbreeding. Their DNA sequences don't —"

"Dad!" Emmet interrupted him.

"We think somebody made them. In a lab," Dr. Doyle said.

10

THE MAN WATCHED THE EVENTS TRANSPIRE ON THE island with rising alarm. His creatures were not behaving normally. The entire plan was for them to scare the boys off the island. He had assumed they could float away in the disabled boat and the creatures would return to the island until he retrieved them. But they were aggressive, pursuing them until Calvin's quick thinking drove them back. What happened?

He admired the boy's cleverness and ingenuity. Fixing the fuel line was something the man didn't expect. There must have been a spare on board. He would have to remember that next time.

Waiting until they disappeared from sight, he started the engine and maneuvered his craft toward the island.

Nearing the shore, he cut the engine and let the boat glide to a stop. He could no longer hear the sound of the motor on *Dragonfly 1*, but he knew Dr. Geaux would send a team out soon to investigate. He pushed the button on the tablet computer and the cage doors on the bow of his boat slid open. The red light on each cage blinked, sending out the beacon. The man held his breath, hoping the homing signal would still work.

A few seconds later, he heard the growls of Hammer and Nails echoing through the trees. Still he waited. There was no further sound from them, and the island and the swamp around it were silent. Birds were no longer visible; even the insects were not chirping. He worried that the hybrids might have left the island and entered the swamp. It would be disastrous. They were not ready to be released.

The man knelt on the deck of his boat and opened a panel that revealed a rifle and a long steel pole with a cable noose at one end. The rifle held tranquilizer darts that should render the creatures unconscious. Of course, he realized just then that he hadn't tested the weapon or the tranquilizer, and had no idea if the darts would penetrate the thick skin of the Pterogators. Trying to capture the creatures with the pole and noose would be dangerous, but not impossible.

His mind raced, dozens of thoughts cascading through it like a waterfall. With Dr. Geaux in possession of the corpse of one of his creatures, his timetable was now artificially advanced. He questioned his decision to let the boys escape. Perhaps that was a mistake. Park officials would be on the alert and even more vigilant. It could interfere with his plans.

The very thought enraged him. These bureaucrats would go to any lengths to stop him from correcting their own incompetence and abuse. They did nothing while the Everglades were destroyed by invasive species and their own inaction. Yet he would be considered the criminal.

Once he recovered Hammer and Nails, it would be time to up his game. If park officials led by Dr. Geaux wanted to push back, then he could push back just as hard.

Or harder. He would see to it that —

Movement in the underbrush interrupted his thoughts. The leaves and branches of the shrubs and saw grass lining the shore of the island shook, and then Hammer and Nails emerged onto the beach. Just like always, they crawled toward the boat and climbed into their cages. He pushed the icon on the tablet and the doors slid silently shut. He let out a long, slow breath.

The amount of time and money he'd invested into these creatures was staggering. And they were only the first stage in his plan to restore not just the Everglades but also the entire South Florida ecosystem. It had taken years of study and nearly all of his wealth to get this far. He couldn't fail now.

The arrival of Dr. Doyle changed things. Once Dr. Geaux recovered the corpse of one of his Pterogators, she would have undoubtedly run DNA tests. The results would show the unique avian and crocodilian DNA of the creature. He should have guessed she would have asked for help on the scientific end. The woman was a complete amateur, in his opinion. How she ever earned a PhD in biology was beyond him.

But Doyle might be a problem. A new set of eyes, someone who specialized in birds of prey, might see how he resequenced the DNA of separate species. He'd figured it out — the secret to making the crossbreeding of two completely different animals possible. One of the greatest scientific breakthroughs of all time and he must keep it a secret. He would have to keep tabs on this Dr. Doyle. There was no way he would let a second-rate bird scientist interfere with his master plan.

He reversed the trolling motor on the boat, waiting until he was in deeper water before he switched on the fan. The boat skimmed across the swamp surface toward his compound. All along the way, he thought of what he would do next if he were given another chance to catch Calvin and the Doyle boy out in the swamp. Maybe they, and what would happen to them, would be the catalyst for the change he so sorely wanted to achieve.

Catalyst.

He smiled. There was that word again.

11

"WHAT DO YOU MEAN 'NOT FROM OUR TIME'? ARE you talking about time travel or something like that?" Emmet asked. Outside the window, darkness was approaching. Dr. Geaux and the others had yet to return to the compound.

"No. Not time travel. That archosaur is real enough. But it's not something that originated in nature. It was hatched in a lab, using recombinant DNA and gene sequencing. There seems to be some gene splicing as well. We have to do more tests. . . ."

"Dad. Slow down. You're doing it again. A recom-bawhata? And sequencasplicing how?" Emmet had been pinned to a chair for a while now by the sleeping Apollo. He lifted the dog down to the floor and stood up. Almost fighting mutant critters had taken all the starch out of the mutt.

"It . . . I . . . sorry. It's fascinating, really. Someone with a tremendous knowledge of molecular and cellular biology has created a hybrid species. In this case, they've recombined the DNA of an alligator and a bird of prey. The result is a creature similar to some types of archosaurs that existed millions of years ago," Dr. Doyle said.

"How is that even possible? They're totally different species," Emmet said.

"True, but for many years, biologists and paleontologists have advanced the theory that modern-day birds are descendants of dinosaurs and prehistoric reptiles. Recent research argues it's more likely they share a common evolutionary ancestor and branched off into different species." Dr. Doyle took another chair from in front of Dr. Geaux's desk and pulled it close, so he sat facing his son.

"But alligators, even fancy, mixed-up genetic freaks like this one, can't climb trees, can they?" Emmet asked.

"No, alligators aren't built to climb trees, but again, this is a different species. It has longer legs and more articulated joints in its limbs. Its claws look made for scaling trunks and branches. And it has folds of skin along its sides, like early archosaurs, that would allow it to glide from branch to branch."

The very idea of one of those beasts floating through the trees made Emmet's skin crawl. He stood up and walked over to look out the window. It had been a long day, and a not-very-good introduction to Florida to boot. He missed Montana.

"Dad," Emmet said. "I don't like it here."

"I know, son," Dr. Doyle said.

"I want to go back to Montana. Can we please go?" Emmet pleaded.

"If only we could, Emmet. But the Fish and Wildlife Service sent me here. Sometimes I can't pick my assignments. And we need me to have a job, so I'm afraid we're kind of stuck in Florida for a while. I'm really sorry you were scared. It must have been terrifying. We'll make sure you don't have to go back into the Everglades," Dr. Doyle said.

Emmet spun around. He tried hard to control himself but he couldn't.

"Dad! You just don't get it! I don't want you out there, either. You haven't seen one of these things up close. I have! They're dangerous. And whoever is doing this doesn't even realize how dangerous. If you go out there and they're on the loose . . . you might . . . it would . . ." Emmet couldn't finish.

"Emmet," Dr. Doyle said after a pause, "it's going to be okay. We've left it floating out there and never really discussed it. What happened to your mom was . . ." Dr.

Doyle didn't get a chance to finish, because Emmet ran out the side door of the office into the parking lot.

"Emmet, come back!" Dr. Doyle shouted from the door.

"NO! I want to go home," Emmet shouted, and ran back up the path toward the dock. It was twilight now, and the sun was setting to the west. The sky was full of reddish light and Emmet ran along the gravel trail. He heard birds calling and insects chirping and it sounded to him like another planet. Montana was quiet and peaceful, with no prehistoric killing machines trying to eat him. Just a few bears, which were far less scary than those flying . . . death merchants. . . . He didn't even know what to call them anymore.

Up ahead he heard the sound of the airboats returning to the dock. Everything sounded foreign to him: the buzz of the swamp, the cry of the cormorants, the mosquito-like whine of the airboat. Not to mention the actual mosquitoes. They were approximately the size of bald eagles, and apparently sent text messages to each other that he was outside and available for feeding. There was no doubt about it — he hated it here. If he could, he'd take his dad's truck and drive himself back to Montana.

He realized that if he kept walking he would run into Calvin and his mom and the rangers. He didn't want that, but he didn't want to go back to the lab, either. His only option was to hide in the underbrush, and that was no option at all, because he didn't know what might be waiting. With his luck, probably a *T. rex*. Or some kind of shark that could live on land that everyone conveniently neglected to tell him about before he moved here.

His indecision cost him, as Dr. Geaux and Calvin and the two rangers spotted him on their way up the path from the dock. Clark and Marcus were big dudes with deep tans, and both were well over six feet tall. They could have passed as brothers, even though Marcus had blond hair. It looked like they did a lot of weight lifting; their arms were roped and coiled with muscles. Emmet hadn't heard them speak yet. He guessed this was why Dr. Geaux chose them for their little committee, because they knew how to keep their mouths shut.

Emmet tried to look casual as they approached, not wanting to give away the fact that he just yelled at his dad and ran out of the lab. Besides, he couldn't think of anything to say or do that didn't sound lame.

"Emmet?" Dr. Geaux said. "What are you doing out here?"

"Nothing. I. Um. Just getting some air," Emmet said.

"I see. Well, we found tracks and other signs from your adventure earlier today," Dr. Geaux said. "And something else." She held up a trash bag, and though Emmet couldn't see what was inside, the way it squished around made him think it was something icky.

"What would that be?" Emmet asked.

"I think we better go inside the lab first," Dr. Geaux said. She stopped for a moment, speaking in low tones to Clark and Marcus. She must have given them some kind of assignment, because without another word they left the group and headed back toward the dock.

"Now I guess we have an idea of what's been driving the gators out of the park," she said. "Come on. Let's get to the lab. There's something I need to show your father, Emmet."

A few minutes later they were back in the lab. Dr. Doyle was still sitting in the chair, where Emmet had left him. Apollo had woken up during Emmet's absence. Apparently unhappy with the accommodations on the floor, he'd crawled up into Dr. Doyle's lap. The little mutt was upside down, all four paws in the air, as Emmet's dad absentmindedly stroked his belly.

"There you are," Dr. Doyle said. He looked at his son but didn't say anything. Still, Emmet noticed the look of relief on his face and felt bad about yelling at his dad. It wasn't his idea to move here, either.

"Apollo, off," Dr. Doyle said as he stood. The dog jumped down from his perch and looked around with his "someone pick me up" face, but found no takers. Disgusted, he jumped back up into the now empty chair and went back to sleep. Archosaur-hunting exhausted him.

"I'm glad you're both still here," Dr. Geaux said. She held up the trash bag. "Let me put this away and then I'd like you both to come over to our place for dinner."

"We don't want to put you to any trouble," Dr. Doyle said.

"Nonsense, I've got some jambalaya that's been slow-cooking all day. It's the least I can do. It's been a rough, long day. Time for some Florida hospitality," she said.

"What about what's in the trash bag?" Emmet asked, suspicious for some reason he couldn't explain.

"It can wait until Monday. Tomorrow is Sunday, and the two of you will need to get your house unpacked. We've done enough work for now," she said.

"Why did you send the rangers back out?" Emmet asked.

"Well, somebody did sabotage your boat. And that makes me plenty angry. Now, it could have been someone unconnected to all of this. There are people, hunters and guides mostly, who pilot all over the Glades. They know our boat, and a few of them don't like some of the decisions I've made as park director. It could be they were playing a prank, thinking it was me out there. But it's a far better chance that whoever did it is connected to these creatures. So Marcus and Clark are going to run a grid search. Look for any sign of who might be behind this," she said.

"But it's dark out," Emmet said.

"Yes, it is. Those two are my best rangers and can keep their mouths shut. They're experienced and know the swamp. And as for the dark, well, sometimes it's better if the person you're looking for doesn't know you're looking." Dr. Geaux smiled and went into the lab, and they heard a door on one of the freezer units open and shut. Then she stuck her head back in the room where the three of them waited.

"Who's hungry?" she asked.

12

EMMET AND DR. DOYLE ARRIVED HOME TO FIND THE rest of their shipment delivered and hastily unloaded in their new house. It was a mess, but Dr. Doyle decided they would deal with it later. They managed to shower and change clothes and stop at a bakery for a cake to take to dinner.

Dr. Geaux lived a couple of miles outside of Florida City in a small development of homes that ran alongside a river. It was a quiet neighborhood with mostly cypress-log homes lining the street. Her house backed up against the river at the end of a cul-de-sac. Emmet finally relaxed when he and his dad arrived there. Like their new home, it was cool inside, with polished wood floors and vaulted ceilings in the main room. The smell of the promised jambalaya wafted over them as they entered.

Emmet had to admit, he was hungry. After what they'd witnessed in the swamp earlier that day, he lost his appetite. Mostly because of the fear. But the delicious aroma convinced him otherwise. Dr. Geaux took the cake from his dad as they exchanged greetings. They followed her into the kitchen, where the smells were even more tempting: fresh bread baking and something with cinnamon.

"Have you ever eaten jambalaya, Emmet?"

"Not that I know of," Emmet said, instantly on guard, as if Dr. Geaux might be attempting to slip something icky past him. Knowing his luck, they were vegetarians or something. *Jambalaya* was probably French for "rutabaga."

"Then you haven't lived. What about you, Benton?" Dr. Geaux said.

"Please, call me Ben. Nobody calls me Benton except for my mother," Dr. Doyle said.

"Ben it is," she said.

Emmet watched the little back and forth like Apollo (who remained at home, fearlessly guarding their belongings) watched a fly buzz about his head. What was this "Ben" business? Nobody called his dad Ben. It was either Dr. Doyle or usually just Doc.

Dr. Geaux stood at the stove, adding seasonings to a big cast-iron stockpot.

"You're going to love it," she said. "Jambalaya is a traditional French-Creole dish, and this particular recipe comes from my grandmother." She scooped up a bit of the jambalaya in the big cooking spoon and turned to offer a taste to Dr. Doyle.

"What do you think?" she asked.

Dr. Doyle tasted the jambalaya and tried very hard not to look like a puckered-up prune. His face went immediately red and his lips curled and uncurled like a fish out of water. Emmet almost laughed out loud. His dad didn't care for spicy food. He nodded and made an "OK" sign with his fingers, covering his mouth with his other hand. There was a large gulping sound as he swallowed down the spoonful of fire.

"That . . . ah . . . it's . . . I . . . never . . . wh . . ." Dr. Doyle stammered.

"Too spicy?" Dr. Geaux asked, smiling.

"No!" Dr. Doyle replied. "Not at all. It's very good. With a delightful kick."

Emmet rolled his eyes.

"Where's Calvin?" he asked.

"Out back, I suspect. In his tree house," Dr. Geaux said. "Go have a look. Right through the living room."

Leaving the kitchen, Emmet wondered what in the world had gotten into his dad. The hallway led to a very spacious living room, two steps down. A large set of

French doors opened onto a back patio, and the backyard ran down to the river. In the darkness, he could just make out a stout wire fence encircling the backyard. Seeing the fence made him think of alligators. Thinking of alligators brought forward the memory of . . . those things who shall not be named . . . from their adventures in the swamp that afternoon. A memory he was desperately trying to suppress.

The backyard was a symphony of sounds as insects and frogs took up their nightly chorus and he wondered if he'd ever get used to that. Montana didn't have as many insects as South Florida and was a lot quieter at night.

There were three large trees in the backyard, though it was too dark to tell what kind they were. Music came from one of them, and Emmet walked toward it. At the base of it he looked up and could see the outline of what indeed looked to be a small house built into the branches.

"Calvin? You up there?" Emmet said.

"Yeah. Come on up," Calvin said.

Emmet didn't see a ladder and he waited, thinking Calvin would maybe lower one down or something. He counted to ten, then twenty, and still nothing happened.

"Calvin?" Emmet said again.

"Yeah?"

"Did you say I could come up?" Emmet asked.

"Yes."

"Well, how?"

He heard Calvin moving around up above. Then he saw the outline of his head appear in the floor of the tree house as dim light filtered through from the interior. It was still plenty dark, though.

"How what?" Calvin asked.

"How do I get up there? A ladder? I don't see one," Emmet said.

"No, you have to climb. Use the branches," Calvin said, as if that explained everything.

Emmet shook his head in disbelief and thought for a moment about just going back inside the house. But a part of him thought the tree house was kind of neat. And he thought he might like to see it. Calvin was turning out to be pretty interesting. He could repair a boat engine with a paper clip, fight off those you-know-whats with a match, and apparently lived in a tree. Emmet could not afford to pass that up.

The first branch was just about head high, so he grasped it and worked his way up into the tree. It wasn't easy, being that this was his first time and it was almost pitch-black out. Slowly, he picked his way through the branches until he reached a square door in the floor of the house. Pushing up on it, he was able to stand up and crawl inside.

"Howdy," Calvin said. He sprawled on a beanbag chair in the far corner. Emmet lowered the hatch closed and stood upright. The structure was about six feet square and eight feet high. The walls were wood halfway up, then screened in above that and open on all four sides. There was a small table in one corner with some books and a lantern sitting on it, the mantle turned down so it gave off a very soft glow. Where Calvin sat, there was a small shelf attached to the wall near his head, holding a small docking station for a music player.

"Hey," Emmet said. "I got to say, this is pretty cool."

"Thanks. I like it up here. Especially in the winter months, when it's cooler."

Calvin was quiet. Not much for conversation, it seemed. Emmet was struggling to try to chat him up.

"Weird day, huh?" he said.

"I guess," Calvin said.

Emmet nearly flipped out. He guessed! Almost eaten alive by prehistoric whatevers and he *guessed*! *Breathe, Emmet*, he told himself. *Don't alienate anyone on your first day.*

"Yeah . . . uh . . . I guess you don't have a day like this very often. Where you meet someone and a couple hours later you go on your first airboat ride and you're almost eaten by a couple of dinosaurs somebody thawed out of the ice somewhere. Then after that you're at their house for jambalaya and discover they live in a tree house and listen to hip-hop," Emmet said. "At least I hope that's not every day."

"I don't live here. It's just where I spend a lot of time. And hip-hop relaxes me. What do you mean, dinosaurs? Those things weren't dinosaurs," Calvin said.

"What? Oh, nothing, really. My dad and I were talking about those critters that attacked us today. The one they examined in the lab has avian and reptile DNA, and my dad said it's almost like whoever bred this thing was trying to create an ancient common ancestor of the alligator and bird. I forget what he called it, the archtarapixalator or something. Honestly, when he's in full-on 'science guy' mode, I breeze out sometimes," Emmet said.

Calvin sat up, the low light showing his face to be interested now.

"Archaeopteryx?" he asked.

"What?" Emmet answered, confused.

"The ancient creature your dad mentioned. Was it the archaeopteryx?"

"I dunno," Emmet said. "Could be. It sounded sort of like that."

"Hmm," Calvin said, lying back in the beanbag.

"What is it?" Emmet asked, telling himself he would not in the least be surprised if Calvin said he held a PhD in paleontology.

"Supposedly, it's the common ancestor of birds and crocodiles. Some scientists believe that birds are descended from reptiles and the archaeopteryx is where the split occurred. One branch of the family tree went on to develop feathers and flight and the other became crocodiles, alligators, and other reptiles," Calvin said.

Emmet paused a second, waiting for Calvin to mention his paleontology degree, but he went silent again. He lay there on the beanbag, completely still, looking up at the roof. He was a riddle to Emmet.

"I don't know about that," Emmet said. "I think we studied it in school once. Maybe. Or it could be I've heard my dad talk about it before. But he and your mom seem to agree that somebody has 'created' those . . . whatever things . . . artificially."

Calvin nodded. "Seems like that would cost a fortune, though. Who would have that kind of money?"

"I guess being rich doesn't keep you from being crazy. Somebody with the money, maybe also had the knowledge. Or enough of both to get by, and thought they'd try and see what they could cook up in a lab. My dad says normal folks are breeding all kinds of weird stuff as it is already. Doesn't take much of a leap to think somebody might try mixing some DNA in a test tube and see what grows out of it."

Calvin might have blinked and nodded, but in the darkness, Emmet couldn't be sure.

Emmet changed the subject. "This is a pretty cool tree house. Did you build it?"

"Yeah. My dad and I. When I was little. We worked on it all one summer. He taught me about tools and building and fixing things. He could make just about anything out of lumber or sticks or bricks or spare auto parts lying around. I like coming up here where I can think," Calvin explained.

Emmet had more questions, but given that he knew Calvin's dad passed away, he didn't want to bring up any bad memories.

"How long do you think it is until dinner?" Calvin asked.

"I don't know. Your mom let my dad taste the jambalaya and he nearly passed out. From the looks of it, it's pretty spicy," Emmet said.

"It is," Calvin said. "She puts about six different kinds of pepper in it, and the sausage is already hot. Maybe we better go save your dad. Get him a glass of milk or something." Calvin stood and opened the trapdoor in the floor, then scrambled through it on his way down the tree.

"Why milk?" Emmet asked as Calvin disappeared below him.

"Milk is what you drink with spicy food to cut the heat. Water just makes it worse," Calvin said, in a manner that implied this was very common knowledge.

"Oh," Emmet said. "I didn't know that." He shrugged himself through the trapdoor and began a careful descent down the tree, all the while wondering what else Calvin knew that he didn't. So far, it seemed like a lot.

Emmet thought the whole dinner was weird. The adults talked about all kinds of things. Recipes, the jambalaya, baseball (Dr. Geaux was a Cubs fan, while Dr. Doyle followed the Orioles) and it was all so strange to Emmet. He didn't remember his dad talking that much with his mom at dinner. He assumed they must have, but couldn't recall it.

And Calvin was certainly not much for small talk. But the conversation between the two adults appeared to freak him out a little, too. His eyes darted back and forth around the table as they talked, almost like he could see the words in the air or something. Emmet was pretty sure he'd never met a boat-piloting, gator-fighting, hip-hop-listening kid like Calvin before.

They ended up staying till almost midnight, and might have stayed longer if Emmet hadn't practically yawned at the top of his lungs five times. Finally, Dr. Doyle caught the hint.

"I guess it's late," he said, glancing at his watch.

Calvin and Emmet were sitting in the living room, unenthusiastically playing video games. Emmet was kind of enjoying the fact that Calvin's mom actually talking to a man was freaking Calvin out a little. But then he remembered it was his dad she was talking to, and that made him feel weird. He jumped up, so as not to miss the chance to get out of there.

"Really? I hadn't noticed," he said. "Thank you for dinner, Dr. Geaux."

"You're welcome, Emmet. You're both welcome," she said.

Dr. Doyle and Dr. Geaux started talking again, and Emmet thought he might fall asleep standing up. Finally they were in the truck, and the next thing Emmet knew he woke up in bed in his new house in a whole new state, surrounded by ferocious, hungry critters.

13

DR. DOYLE AND EMMET SPENT THE NEXT DAY, SUNDAY, unpacking all of their household goods. It was hard, hot work, and Emmet despaired, realizing the heat was only going to get worse as the spring and summer progressed. He didn't know if he could survive it. As he worked, he imagined all the different methods he and Apollo could use to return to Montana on their own.

He'd come up with thirty-seven different ways so far. His favorite required a bus trip to Disney World, where he would find a car with Montana license plates and let them tow him back by secretly hooking his skateboard to the bumper. He pictured Apollo in a tiny helmet and goggles and chuckled. Maybe it would come to that.

When he and his father finally opened the last box

it was well after dark and Emmet was exhausted. His body clock was completely out of whack with the time change, the long drive, and the almost being eaten. Now he was thinking about school tomorrow. Bad enough being the new kid. New kid in the middle of the year was an even worse experience. He'd almost rather venture back into the swamp and look for those . . . no, he wouldn't.

Monday morning he was jumpy as a cat. He was attending the same middle school as Calvin, so at least he would know someone. His dad was going to drive him to school so he didn't have to ride the bus with a bunch of strangers the first day. This was the second time Emmet enrolled at a new school without his mom there to help him through it. At least in Montana he'd started at the beginning of the year. But no matter where they moved or how difficult it was for him, she'd always made it easier. In order to not deal with it, he stalled and lingered over breakfast.

"Emmet, I know this is probably the last thing you want to do. And really, I wish . . ." Dr. Doyle's words trailed off and his voice cracked, and for a moment Emmet thought he saw tears in his father's eyes, but pulled himself together, as if realizing this wasn't about him.

"I wish your mom were here because I know it's hard on you, moving around so much, and always being the new kid. Your mom had a way about her. She understood things. When stuff like this happened, she always knew the right things to say to make you feel better. I . . . I'm not . . . good at that like she was. I just want you to know, I'll do whatever I can to make it easy on you. I promise." Dr. Doyle looked at Emmet and winked.

It made Emmet feel a little better. Not completely; even at twelve, he understood that his mom and dad were different people. Parents weren't the same. When his mom was alive he knew they both loved him, but they were just different. His mom was a free spirit who liked loud music, the outdoors, and art. His dad was a scientist, thoughtful and measured, and a little more buttoned down. It wasn't his dad's fault his mom died, and he knew it wasn't his dad's idea to be transferred to the Everglades. But knowing that didn't make it any easier.

"Thanks, Dad," he said. "I suppose I'll get used to it. There's only a few months of school left, anyway."

Dr. Doyle nodded. "Thanks for being so understanding. But, Emmet, in order for you to be the new kid in school you actually have to be *in* the school. So we need to pick up the pace, or we're going to be late. After work, I'm going to —" He was interrupted by the sound of a car pulling into the driveway.

Dr. Doyle went to the front door. "It's Rosa . . . Dr. Geaux and Calvin," he said.

Emmet heard the car doors slam and his dad inviting them in. Dr. Geaux was dressed in a National Park Service uniform and Calvin was wearing khaki cargo shorts and a purple polo shirt. He was also carrying what might have been the biggest book bag Emmet had ever seen strapped to his back. No doubt he carried an inflatable airboat, a cello, and a collapsible tree house inside it. Emmet thought that if Calvin ever fell over onto his back, he might never get up.

"This is a pleasant surprise," Dr. Doyle said, smiling. It was a goofy smile, Emmet thought. His dad just met Dr. Geaux, and any time he was around her he got all weird. Emmet couldn't figure it out, but it bugged him.

"Good morning to both of you," she said. "I thought since it was Emmet's first day, Calvin and I could give him a lift. I know the principal and the office staff at the school very well. We do a lot of Field and Environmental Club activities for the district at the park. This way Calvin can show him the ropes. You know, the important stuff, like where the boys' room is, the cafeteria, and whatnot."

"That's very nice of you," Dr. Doyle said. "Emmet, what do you think? Want to ride with them, or shall I drive you?"

Emmet shrugged. "It's okay, I guess."

"Perfect," Dr. Geaux said. "I also came over this morning because I needed to make sure we're all on the same page regarding what happened Saturday. We can't let anyone but the four of us, and my two rangers, know what we've found. There was another story in the morning papers about alligators migrating out of the Glades. A fifteen-footer showed up outside a day-care-center fence in Homestead. Sent the parents into a frenzy, and people are asking more questions. I suspect I'll have a stack of messages from the news media when I get to the office. I just want to make sure we zip our lips until we figure out who is behind this."

Emmet and Dr. Doyle looked at each other and nodded.

"Of course. We won't say anything to anyone," Dr. Doyle said.

"Pinky swear?" Dr. Geaux said, holding out her pinky finger.

Emmet couldn't help it, but she made him laugh.

"Pinky swear," Emmet said.

"All right. Ben, I'll see you at park HQ. Emmet, get your gear and let's roll. I think you're going to like your school. And Ben, you better bring that adorable mutt along with you today."

Apollo stood up from where he lay sprawled on the kitchen floor and wagged his tail. Sometimes Emmet was certain the dog could understand human speech.

"Will do," Dr. Doyle said. "Have a good day, son. Tell me all about it when I get home." He knew enough not to embarrass Emmet by hugging him, so he held out his fist for a fist bump. Emmet silently groaned but bumped fists with his dad, anyway. He made a mental note to ask his dad later to please not try acting hip in front of other people. He was really bad at it.

Leaving the house, he couldn't help but think how Dr. Geaux and Calvin's arrival already made his day feel routine. He wasn't sure how it happened, but he found himself less stressed out about starting over in a new place. Even his dad had seemed more relaxed.

As they climbed into the car, a bull alligator bugled from the canal behind their house. It reminded Emmet of the previous day, and a small bit of tension tightened along the muscles in his back and shoulders. He would leave it to his father and Dr. Geaux to deal with the weird alligator problem. As far as Emmet Doyle was concerned, he might have to live here for now, but he never had to go back into the Everglades.

If only that had turned out to be true.

14

HIDDEN AWAY IN HIS COMPOUND, THE MAN HAD stared at the computer screen for the last dozen hours, watching the data roll by. Given the strange behavior of Hammer and Nails on the island yesterday, his entire experiment was now called into question. He'd spent the last two days poring over his research, pausing only for a few hours of sleep.

What had gone wrong? In his controlled experiments, the beasts always performed magnificently, even by-passing mammals or other easier prey and zeroing in directly on the snakes. But he had lost one to the Park Service, and Hammer and Nails had not acted as he'd anticipated. The intention of releasing them on the island had been to have them scare the two boys and create the false impression in Dr. Geaux's mind that the swamp was now full of this new species. Knowing the danger to public safety, she would have no choice but to shut down the park, and this would allow his creatures to eradicate the snakes without human interference.

But Hammer and Nails had turned aggressive. Instead of merely announcing their presence, they attacked. There was no doubt they would have overwhelmed the boys if the quick thinking of Calvin had not saved them. Something went wrong, but what? And why had the other specimen escaped and then died, its corpse falling into the hands of his enemy, allowing them to examine it?

He stood and rubbed his eyes and stretched, massaging the sore muscles in his back. As he paced back and forth in front of his workstation, the data streams poured through his mind. No one understood how remarkable his achievement was. Using recombinant DNA, mixing the DNA of two distinct species into one organism, he had managed to create an animal that would be the salvation of the Everglades.

He had played back the recording of Dr. Doyle and Dr. Geaux's autopsy. It was impossible to believe how quickly Dr. Doyle zeroed in on what he had done. Perhaps he was much smarter than he appeared. While they worked and Doyle studied the lab results, he told Dr. Geaux that the DNA strands and tissue samples, as well as the morphology of the creature, pointed to a prehistoric pterosaur, or an offshoot of an archaeopteryx-type dinosaur. Perhaps this creature had been found in a more preserved state, much like the mastodons and wooly mammoths that had been found in parts of Russia, preserved in ice. If the preservation of the carcass was good enough to allow extraction of enough tissue to form a complete DNA strand, such a creature could easily be cloned.

When the man heard Dr. Doyle's explanation to Dr. Geaux, he sat there, dumbstruck. For he had described almost exactly how his Pterogators had come to life. It was a little more complicated than that; he was brilliant, after all. But Dr. Doyle had cut right to the heart of his work. This could be a problem.

With the right amounts of money and knowledge, cloning was almost becoming commonplace. But cloning prehistoric creatures was the stuff of movies and comic books. Because finding a complete DNA sequence in a fossil or frozen remains had proved nearly impossible. But with enough money and luck, he had found everything he needed.

The man did not expect anyone to comprehend the brilliance of his research. Yet Dr. Doyle made a leap of intuition right away. This could prove troublesome. Once Dr. Geaux and Dr. Doyle completed their study, they would begin following the trail backward. And though he had covered his tracks well, there was no guarantee that he wouldn't be discovered.

What he had done was a step beyond cloning. He had taken two distinct but evolutionarily distantly related species, the alligator and the great gray owl, and mapped their DNA. With a specimen of DNA from a prehistoric crocodilian, he had taken the best attributes of both species and combined them into his new crocodilians. And since both gators and owls were hatched from eggs, it was easier to keep experimenting until he created the exact specimen he was looking for.

From there, as they grew, he trained them to hunt snakes. Birds of prey, such as falcons, could be trained to hunt, and his creatures were no different. Falcons were taught to hunt doves, for example. With proper training, they focused on doves at the exclusion of other food sources. After three years of work, he had achieved the same results. His creations were bred and trained to focus on pythons and boa constrictors.

And he was now almost ready to let them loose and bring the ecosystem here back into balance.

At least he'd thought so. Until yesterday, when the boys had somehow interfered.

The boys.

Could that be it? His trials in the lab had used many different mammals, birds, and reptiles to dissuade or distract his creatures from tracking and killing snakes. In every instance they bypassed these animals and focused solely on the snakes.

But they had never encountered other humans. Could that be it? Had the presence of the two boys thrown off Hammer's and Nails's senses?

An interesting hypothesis. It would need testing. And to test it properly he would need a subject. And he knew exactly whom he would use. But doing so would create pressure and heat if the person came up missing. He needed to clear the park of civilians at the very least. Then his experiment could proceed, hopefully before his subject's disappearance was discovered.

Sitting back down at his workstation, he typed out an email. It was time to put the South Florida area on notice. He was responsible for the alligators, birds, and other creatures that were migrating out of the park and causing havoc in the nearby cities and towns. When he was finished, he attached a file of the video of Hammer and Nails attacking and devouring a python. The email would be anonymous and untraceable, bounced around from a dozen different servers and IP addresses. A new day was about to dawn.

He pushed send, and the email was on its way to every media outlet in South Florida. Then he pulled up the video and audio feeds of Park HQ. If he was lucky, he would have a subject for his test very soon. The man leaned back in his chair and smiled.

He had signed the email "Dr. Catalyst."

15

THERE WAS NOTHING NEW IN EMMET'S FIRST DAY AT Tasker Middle School in Florida City. At least, nothing he hadn't experienced what seemed like a thousand times before. Everyone stared at him. Some kids were friendly. A few made wisecracks about his appearance. There were unfriendly kids, but most were overwhelmingly ambivalent and ignored him.

Dr. Geaux dropped them off at the front door in her Buick. She wished them well and drove away without making a big deal about it. Emmet decided that, for another kid's mother, she was pretty okay. His mom had always done the same thing, simply saying "Goodbye. Have a great day," and driving off. Not "Don't worry, Emmet, you'll make friends easily." Or "Why, you'll be up to speed in no time," or "Before long you'll be the principal, Emmet!" and other such annoying phrases. His mom avoided all the "good parenting" and "esteem building" clichés that usually only made him feel worse.

She just drove him up to the school, said "Have a good one," and left. Eventually, Emmet came to realize that this was his mom's way of telling him he could do it on his own. He didn't need any false praise or supportive banter. It might be tough. Certainly not easy. But she believed in him. Dr. Geaux had essentially just done the same thing, and he couldn't help himself, but he liked her even more for it.

Everyone knows that middle school is an obstacle course of social hierarchies. Emmet never usually hung out with the cool kids. He was okay at sports but not a jock by any stretch. Nor did he fall in with the brainiacs or the music and drama geeks. Usually he landed in the middle somewhere, friendly enough to get along with most anyone.

But after meeting Calvin this weekend, the boat-piloting, swamp-guiding, tree-house-loving, predagator-fighting, hip-hop-listening superkid, he was dying to know where Calvin stood in the social strata at Tasker Middle School.

Emmet was surprised to find that Calvin was part of a small but interesting group of friends. They weren't jocks, or what most observers would consider popular, but they were . . . normal. Mostly. And Emmet had to admit they were a fun group.

Riley was a tall, slender strawberry blond who wore "smart girl" glasses with black frames. At lunchtime, it took Emmet about three minutes to realize Riley had a huge crush on Calvin. Calvin was, of course, completely oblivious to her feelings.

There was a bigger, strong-looking kid everyone called Stuke. It was short for Stukaczowski, which Emmet didn't think he would ever learn to pronounce. His red hair was buzz-cut, and a galaxy of freckles splashed across his nose and cheeks.

Raeburn was medium height with long, shiny black hair reaching to the middle of her back. Calvin told Emmet later that she was a Seminole, and came to Tasker Middle School from the reservation because she was a math and science whiz.

They all welcomed Emmet to their table at lunch. They laughed and joked with him, making him feel less like a fifth wheel. Surprisingly, Stuke did most of the talking, asking Emmet all kinds of questions about Montana. Did he ski? Snowboard? Had he ever seen a grizzly bear?

Emmet liked them, but was dying to ask all of them if they knew that Calvin piloted airboats, fought mysterious ferocious beasts, and chilled out to hip-hop in his tree house.

Of course, he couldn't say anything about the strange creatures, and he found it harder to keep quiet about it than he'd thought. And he didn't want to mention their airboat trip, because that would let the others know that he and Calvin were out in the swamp; it would lead to further discussion, and he was afraid something might slip out.

"How come you moved to Florida all the way from Montana?" Riley asked.

"My dad works for Fish and Wildlife. He's a bird expert. He's working with the Everglades Park HQ on something about the migratory and habitat analysis of the red-breasted something or other and how it blah, blah, blah, blah, snore . . ." Emmet said.

This got a good laugh from the others at the table, even Calvin. Emmet was pretty sure this was the first time he'd seen him laugh. He really did. For at least 1.9 seconds. A chuckle at the very least.

"Sounds exciting," Raeburn said.

"Oh yeah! Especially when . . . no. It's never exciting," Emmet said.

Everyone laughed again, and Raeburn reached out and poked him on the arm. Emmet thought that was weird. Not bad weird. But she seemed to think he was funny. He'd never thought of himself that way. He would have to think on this "laughing at his jokes, poking him in the arm" thing later.

"Since your dad works for Fish and Wildlife, have you heard about all the critters crawlin' out of the Glades?" Stuke asked.

"Yeah," Calvin answered for Emmet. "Weird."

That Calvin, Emmet thought. *What a conversationalist.*

"They found a big gator next to a day-care center the other day," Stuke went on. "If it weren't for the fence, it might have been snackin' on some of the munchkins."

"Stuke!" Riley said.

"What?" he said. "It's true. My dad's a cop, Emmet. He's been getting all kinds of nuisance calls. Maybe your dad will figure out why all the birds and gators are leaving the swamp."

Emmet tried with every ounce of self-control he possessed not to look at Calvin, and failed. It was only a quick glance, and Calvin kept his stone face perfectly in place, but Emmet felt like everyone was watching him and thought the best tactic was to change the subject.

"So, where exactly is the science lab?" he asked. "It's next on my schedule."

"Oh, you got Dr. Newton," Raeburn said.

"You have a science teacher named Newton?" Emmet asked.

They all looked at him blankly.

"Is the English teacher Mr. Dickens?"

Each of them smiled.

"Okay, lame. Sorry. Sometimes I can't help myself. I

have Dr. Newton. Is that bad?" Emmet was suddenly concerned.

"Oh, not bad, necessarily, just . . ." Raeburn said.

"Just what?" Emmet insisted.

"You'll see!" She smiled and poked him in the arm again. This time Emmet noticed her piercing green eyes. The whole table was snickering now, even Calvin.

"Dr. Newton," Riley said, shaking her head.

"Yeah," said Stuke.

"What? What about Dr. Newton?" Emmet pleaded. But the bell rang. Everyone stood and gathered up their lunch trash.

"I'll show you where the lab is," Raeburn said to Emmet.

Emmet glanced at Calvin.

"Dudes. Come on. You have a science teacher named Newton? That's at least mildly humorous. And why are you all acting like I'm going to get my pants set on fire or something?" Emmet was getting a little nervous.

Calvin just shrugged. "Got to go. See you outside after school. My mom is picking us up."

Raeburn walked Emmet to the lab.

"No one is going to let me in on the secret?" Emmet asked her.

She smiled and poked him in the arm. Again.

"You'll see," she said as she strolled down the hallway.

16

DR. CATALYST STOOD INSIDE THE LABORATORY OF HIS compound, studying the new batch of hatchlings inside the tank. Only four weeks old, they were already approaching eighteen inches in length. While the embryos gestated inside their eggs, he'd injected them with a series of growth hormones. A normal alligator would take years to achieve a mature length of up to fifteen feet. His method advanced the process so that they would reach ten to twelve feet in a matter of months. At that size they would be more than capable of hunting and destroying a large snake.

With a large pair of thick leather gloves, he lifted one of the hatchlings from the tank. Despite their size, their teeth and claws were razor-sharp. Carefully he placed the small creature inside a tank on the other side of the room. This one held half a dozen small boa constrictors, none more than two feet in length. The tank was one hundred and fifty gallons in capacity, and the snakes were curled in a ball at the end. Dr. Catalyst placed the hatchling at the opposite end of the tank.

It lifted its neck. There was slight movement around its nostrils as it sniffed the air. Its eyes focused on the ball of snakes and it took a small leap; the folded wings between its legs stretched out, and it glided through the air, landing feetfirst on the pile of snakes. The boas were frantic to escape. Some tried to slither away, while others wrapped themselves around the hybrid, attempting to strangle it.

The snakes were no match for even the smaller beast. With gruesome efficiency, it bit down on the body of one of the boas, while its claws tore at another. The remaining snakes tried to flee the cage, but there was no escape. Within minutes the small hybrid killed them all, just as it'd been designed to.

Dr. Catalyst finished his study of the data he collected on Hammer's and Nails's behavior on the island with the Geaux and Doyle boys. The collars they wore contained small chips, which recorded the creatures' vital signs when they were out of the lab. Nothing in the data indicated a problem. He attributed it to an anomaly. There could be no other explanation. In the end, he decided not to be concerned about it. They had both been in the swamp several times since the incident and performed as expected.

Returning to his control room, he turned one of his monitors to a local Miami TV station. Since his email was sent, the press, predictably, had worked itself into a frenzy of alarm. The video of Hammer and Nails destroying a python was replayed over and over again on television and hundreds of websites. A quick search showed that the video went viral, with millions of views. And Dr. Catalyst was now sending the news outlets regular email updates, warning the people of South Florida that he intended to take back and restore the Everglades. From now on, citizens were to enter the park at their own risk.

One of the local channels was now showing an interview of Dr. Geaux at Park HQ. The reporters peppered her with questions. She did her best to remain calm and professional, but Dr. Catalyst was a master at reading people. He could see the lines of concern etched into her face as she struggled to reassure the public that the danger was minimal.

"Any wild animal should automatically be given a wide berth. Here in Florida, we inhabit the homes of countless wild creatures. Contact between humans and animals is, at times, inevitable. If we remain calm, and call upon our local police, animal control, and first responders, we can help ensure that neither animal nor human is injured," she patiently explained.

Another reporter shouted a question about the tape of the two strange creatures and asked for her opinion on the statements of the so-called "Dr. Catalyst."

Dr. Geaux paused before answering, running a hand through her curly black hair.

"We are examining the video, but have every reason to believe it is a hoax. Alligators and pythons are apex predators who generally do not feed on each other. We believe whoever sent this video is taking advantage of an unusual migratory behavior of some species and has obviously used computer animation to dramatize an event to make it appear that these creatures are the reason we are seeing several species on the move in the Glades. This event has clearly been staged to create hysteria and panic. Giving in to that panic only allows this individual to gain the notoriety he or she seeks. The Everglades belong to the people, and will remain open for their enjoyment. We will, of course, advise caution to all who visit the park. But we believe this 'Dr. Catalyst' is a fraud attempting to perpetuate some type of hoax for reasons yet to be determined. The National Park Service is cooperating with state and local agencies, and we expect Dr. Catalyst will be exposed as a charlatan very soon."

Reporters shouted more questions, but Dr. Geaux did

not answer, instead walking away from the assembled media and returning to her office. Dr. Catalyst slammed his fist on the console in frustration.

Fraud!

Charlatan!

How dare that woman? Dr. Geaux deliberately lied to the people! She possessed a carcass of one of his creations and knew exactly the greatness of his achievement. She wished to keep the park open, did she?

He stormed to a cabinet along the wall, opening it to reveal a rack of tranquilizer rifles. Hefting one, he sighted down the barrel. It was time to raise the stakes.

Fraud.

"We'll see about that," he said to the empty room.

17

EMMET HAD NEVER EXPERIENCED A FIRST DAY WITH A teacher like the one he had with Dr. Newton. Everyone sat at highboy lab tables in hard-back stools where they could conduct their experiments. Emmet wasn't sure if he got off on the wrong foot with Dr. Newton or not. In fact, after about five minutes he wasn't sure if even Dr. Newton knew where he stood.

But first, he was assigned a seat. His lab partner was apparently going to be a kid named Jimmy Johnston.

"Everybody calls me Double J," he said as Emmet sat down on the stool next to him.

"My name is Emmet," Emmet said, trying to get comfortable in the high-back chair.

"Cool. Where you from?" Double J asked.

"Moved here from Montana," he said.

"You like science?"

Emmet shrugged. "I guess it's okay."

"I don't," Double J said. He was taller than Emmet, already close to six foot, which was tall for a sixth grader. He was about as big around as a #2 pencil and his long hair was an indeterminate brown color pulled back in a ponytail. The weather outside was already pushing eighty degrees, but Double J wore a thick leather jacket, blue jeans with a chain wallet attached to his belt, and thick black army boots.

"Oh, well. What classes do you like?" It was probably a good idea to try to be polite to someone dressed like a biker. Even if he was a sixth grader.

"Lunch," Double J said, putting his head down on the table atop his crossed arms and falling immediately to sleep. Emmet jumped when Dr. Newton called his name.

"Emmet Doyle!" he said, from the front of the room.

"Yes . . . sir," Emmet replied with hesitation.

"Class, meet our newest student, Emmet Doyle," Dr. Newton said. There were a few muttered "hi's" but the response was otherwise underwhelming.

Dr. Newton strolled up to Emmet's table, giving him a good looking-over, like he might be buying a horse or something. He was medium height, a little on the heavy side. His long hair stuck out all over his head like he'd been shocked, and he wore a tweed sport coat over a green T-shirt that said I SUPPORT GREENPEACE in white letters. His new science teacher also wore Birkenstock sandals with socks. To Emmet, this made him immediately suspect.

"You're from Montana," Dr. Newton said.

Emmet wasn't sure if it was a question or a statement. So he just nodded yes.

"What did you do there?" Dr. Newton asked.

"Um. Snowboarded, went to school, I —"

Dr. Newton cut him off. "Snowboarded! You know, ski resorts are bad for the environment. They destroy the habitat. What do your parents do for a living? Do they work for oil companies?"

Emmet wasn't sure what was going on. It felt like he was on trial.

"I only have my dad . . . he's a scientist. He works for the U.S. Fish and Wildlife Service. He's here to work in the Everglades. He —"

"The Everglades. *Pfft*. The government is ruining the Everglades. They have no backbone. Won't stand up to the corporations who'd just as soon pave over the Glades and build condos." Dr. Newton stared at Emmet.

Emmet was pretty sure you couldn't pave a swamp, but he kept that remark to himself.

"I wouldn't know about that. He's an avian specialist. He's working with the Park Service on migratory —"
Again, Emmet didn't get a chance to finish.

At the mention of "avian specialist," Dr. Newton's demeanor suddenly changed. It was subtle, but he stood up a little straighter and his eyes drilled into Emmet with an intense stare.

"An avian specialist, you say. What kind of birds?" Dr. Newton asked. Truthfully, it was more barked than asked. The guy was making Emmet nervous and he didn't know why.

"Raptors. H-he works on how —" Emmet stammered, but was immediately interrupted.

"Raptors? What is he doing here? Trying to figure out how the government and the lobbyists are killing off the eagle and osprey populations?"

"Uh. No. At least, I don't think . . . he doesn't . . ." Emmet got all tongue-tied and didn't know what he was supposed to say, desperate to find the words that would send Dr. Newton on his way. He felt like an ant being studied by a praying mantis.

"Hmm. Well, I'd like to meet your father sometime. And learn more exactly about what it is he thinks he's up to in the Everglades. Helping the raptor population? I seriously doubt it. But welcome to Tasker Middle School and Florida City. Luckily for the environment, you can't snowboard here." Dr. Newton kicked the table leg and Double J came awake with a start.

"Suntans!" he said out loud, having just been woken up without warning.

"Wake up, Mr. Johnston, or you'll have plenty of time to work on your tan when you flunk out of school." Dr. Newton handed Emmet a textbook he'd tucked under his arm. "This is your text. We're on chapter thirty, the study of the ecosystems of coral reefs and the marine life they support. Try to keep up."

He spun on his sandaled heel and stalked to the front of the room. As he did so, Double J coughed an uncomplimentary word about Dr. Newton into his hand.

"Sounds like you have a cold, Mr. Johnston," Dr. Newton said. "Perhaps a few days' suspension will allow you the time to get healthy again."

Double J said nothing, returning his head to the table. Emmet could swear that in four seconds or less he was already snoring softly. He'd never seen anyone fall asleep so fast.

After meeting Dr. Newton, he was glad there was only one more period to go in his first day at Tasker Middle School. It was going to be a long, long time until summer vacation.

18

THE FIRST WEEK OF SCHOOL FELT LIKE A YEAR TO EMMET. The academic part was fine. And he actually liked Calvin's friends. But Dr. Newton was making his life a little miserable. After their first encounter, he made a point of seeking Emmet out every day. He quizzed Emmet about his father and if he was working with Dr. Geaux on the strange migrations of the animals in the park. It was all over the news, he constantly reminded everyone in the class, and the media knew the government was behind it. The government kept secrets, blah, blah, blah. And if that wasn't bad enough, he just kept piling on the homework and seemed to take exception to anyone who said anything even remotely controversial about the environment, spouting into a long lecture. Emmet thought he might be one of those people who would be happiest if everyone lived in huts and subsisted on a diet of twigs and bark. And wore Birkenstocks with wool socks. Emmet just couldn't get past that.

The two of them rode the bus to Calvin's house after school. They would wait there until their parents got home from work, and a couple of times they went out for dinner, or Calvin would heat up something in the microwave.

So far Calvin's tree house had become Emmet's favorite place. The two of them got into the habit of doing their homework up there, and the setting was very relaxing. The breezes up in the trees cut the heat and it was more comfortable there.

It was Thursday, nearly the end of Emmet's first week at Tasker, and it was amazing how much homework he was given, especially in science class.

"What is the deal with this Dr. Newton guy?" Emmet asked Calvin.

"The Newt? I don't know. He's a bit odd, I guess," Calvin said.

It took superhuman effort on Emmet's part to not point out that Calvin spent most of his time in a tree house and carried the world's biggest backpack, and yet he just described someone as "a bit odd."

"Duh. He walks around all the time like his hair is on fire. Man, he hates the government. Gives me all kinds of grief about my dad, who just studies birds. And why is he a doctor?" Emmet said.

"I don't know. He has a PhD in biology or something. The word is, he comes from a wealthy family that made all their money building hotels or something in Miami. There're rumors he doesn't have any other relatives and he didn't want to do anything but teach science in middle school. He's into all kinds of environmental causes around here. 'Save the Manatees' and 'Save the Everglades' and 'Save the Snowbirds,'" Calvin said. "He gets into it with my mom sometimes. She just thinks he's kind of a harmless crank. Feels guilty about his family tearing everything up, so now he wants to preserve everything."

Emmet's head snapped around. "Did you just make a joke?"

"I don't think so," Calvin said.

"Yeah, you did. Good job. You said 'Save the Snowbirds' and thought I wouldn't catch it. Anyway, Dr. Greenpeace Newton seems to have it in for me."

Calvin shook his head. "I don't think so. He's tough and can be opinionated, and gets a little soapboxy about the environment, but he's actually a pretty great teacher. He's on you a lot right now because you're new and he's challenging you. Seeing what you're made of. You'll learn a lot. I did last year."

"How come you don't have him this year?" Emmet asked.

"Like I said, he's involved in a lot of environmental causes. He's got money and that gets him on boards and committees, and he makes big donations and doesn't see eye to eye with my mom very much. I can't say he was ever unfair to me, and I got an A in the class, but he actually suggested I have Ms. Susskind this year to avoid any appearance that he might have a conflict of interest. The whole thing was his idea. Like I said, tough, but pretty fair."

"Well, right now he's making me feel like I'm personally responsible for the decline of the grizzly bear population in Montana because I went snowboarding every once in a while. Doesn't even know the grizz are on the way back," Emmet groused.

"That's Dr. Newt. But you'll like him by the end of the semester. Trust me," Calvin said. Emmet was skeptical.

They were quiet a while as they worked. Emmet observed that just as in most everything else he did, Calvin was a serious student. But before long the conversation between them inevitably turned to Dr. Catalyst, who was all over the media in South Florida the last few days.

"Phony or real?" Emmet flipped on his back, tired of his science textbook.

"What?" Calvin asked.

"Dr. Catalyst. Do you think he's real, or is he a fake?"

"He's real. *Somebody* is sending those emails and videos."

Emmet sighed. "Not what I meant. Do you think there is just this one guy behind making those freak-a-gators?"

"The what?"

"Calvin, I've only known you a short time, but sometimes I think you do this on purpose. You know very well what I'm talking about. Those things that tried to munch on us in the swamp. My dad says the avian DNA strain matches an owl from Asia. Or someplace that starts with an *A*, maybe Alabama, I don't know. Anyway, it's a really big, bad bird of prey. So somebody mixed up owl and alligator DNA into a hybrid species that would take a lot of money and knowledge to create. So my question is, Dr. Catalyst . . . is he behind it, or is he just the front man for a group of extremists who want to take back the Everglades?"

"Oh," Calvin said. "I don't know."

"You don't know?"

"No. I haven't really thought about it."

"Seriously? You haven't thought about it? It's all over the news. People are packing up and moving away until the police catch this guy. Regular alligators are practically riding bicycles down the street because something is driving them out of the swamp. Stuke says his dad is working overtime every day answering police calls from people who think they have a gator in their chimney or their glove compartment, and you 'haven't thought about it'?"

Calvin shrugged. "Not really. Down here in South Florida we're used to eco-protestors. People make all kinds of demands when it comes to the environment. Some want to close the park completely. Others want to make everyone move out of South Florida so it can return to its natural state. This guy just seems like the next in a long line."

"But what about the almost-ate-us-gators? Everybody is running around saying they're not real. It's all a computer-generated hoax to scare people. But they are real. We've seen them, so somebody definitely created those things. Don't you think a person like that is dangerous?"

Calvin shrugged again. Emmet was starting to think a shrug was Calvin's primary response to everything. *Hey, Calvin, your hair's on fire.* Shrug. *Hey, Calvin, look at the size of that cat!* Shrug. *Calvin, here you are . . . one million dollars, tax free.* Shrug.

"Whoever he is, he's right about the invasive species," Calvin said. "The snakes have just about killed off most of the small mammals. You hardly see a swamp fox or opossum or even a raccoon when you're out there these days."

"Wait. Are you saying some guy inventing his own animals is okay? Animals with big scary teeth? Remember, that one time, WHEN THEY ALMOST ATE US?"

Calvin, no surprise, shrugged. "No, I'm not saying what he's doing is right. My dad used to talk a lot about the balance of nature. And now that balance has been upset. My mom and other park officials have been trying to come up with a solution to save the mammals and birds being wiped out by pythons. It's been nothing but frustrating for them. Restoring the balance is never easy once it's been altered. People let these big snakes loose, or they escape and no one realizes the damage they can do. They don't have any natural predators, and all the species they eat here haven't adapted to their presence."

"So it's okay for Dr. Cataracts to make a monster in a lab to fix the problem? They wrote a famous book about that once. It was called *Frankenstein*. Didn't work out so well," Emmet said. "Plus, a couple of his 'solutions' tried to have us for brunch!"

"Well, I didn't say that. . . ." Calvin said.

Emmet saw that winning an argument with Calvin would be difficult at best. So he changed the subject.

"You know, Riley likes you," he said. This time Calvin's head snapped up from his homework, his dark eyes boring into Emmet.

"She . . . you . . . What did you say?" Calvin stammered. He didn't shrug this time.

"Riley. She likes you," Emmet said, pretending to be very interested in his homework.

"No she doesn't," Calvin insisted.

"Does too."

"Does not."

"Does too."

"What are you, six? How long are you going to keep doing this?" Calvin asked.

It was the first time Emmet ever saw him so agitated.

"Does too!" Emmet said, smiling.

"She doesn't know I like her," Calvin said. "I mean — she doesn't like me!"

"Aha!" Emmet said. "I knew you knew it. And you like her back."

Calvin stood up and paced back and forth in the small space of the tree house.

"You can't tell . . . you better . . . I don't want her to . . ." Calvin was really flustered. Emmet was about to speak, when they heard the sound of a car in the driveway.

"As much as I'm enjoying this moment and would give almost anything to prolong it, that's probably my dad. Time to go," Emmet said. He gathered up his books and stuffed them into his book bag, then climbed down the tree with Calvin sputtering behind him.

19

DR. CATALYST MOVED THROUGH THE SWAMP IN NEAR-
total concealment. He wore a specially camouflaged
jumpsuit, which kept him hidden in the shadows and
allowed him to blend in with the flora of the Glades. The
suit was a unique design. It was waterproof, and two
small solar panels attached to the shoulders powered an
air circulation system. As the heat rose from his body, the
suit sent coolant into tiny vessels through the fabric next
to his skin. It kept him from overheating and also made
him harder to detect by any infrared or heat-seeking
devices. His face was covered by sophisticated eye gear
used by military Special Forces units. They looked like
swimming goggles, but could work as binoculars as well,
and were controlled by a thin panel attached to his wrist.

All week he'd been waiting for the right opportunity. Dr. Geaux had called him a fraud and a charlatan, and so far refused his demands to close the Everglades. She gave him no choice. It was time to up the stakes.

He spent most of the day watching the park headquarters through his hidden cameras, observing the comings and goings of the personnel. Dr. Geaux deployed teams of rangers in airboats and doubled the patrols combing the swamp, sending her officers to every inlet, stream, creek, and copse of trees looking for anything unusual.

Dr. Geaux was cautious, making sure her people were always paired in teams, and insisted they maintain regular radio contact with Park Ops. All week he watched airboats leave the headquarters facility and never once did less than two rangers depart in a single boat. His microphones in the briefing room supplied him the grid coordinates the teams would search each day. He'd also planted tracking devices on the boats weeks prior, in anticipation that they might be useful. Now he could track their locations from the tablet console on his own craft.

He'd shadowed some of the teams in his boat as they searched, looking for any sign of him or his creatures. Though he had no plans to release any of his animals until Dr. Geaux closed the park, so far she'd refused. Now there was no choice but to force her hand.

Early that morning, Dr. Geaux and Dr. Doyle dispatched the search teams. After completing further study of the recovered Pterogator corpse, they also left the lab and headed into the swamp aboard an airboat. Thinking this might be the chance he was looking for, he followed them.

For a reason yet undetermined, they returned to the very island where Hammer and Nails encountered the boys the previous weekend. The water was lower this time, so they anchored their airboat and waded ashore. Dr. Catalyst maneuvered his boat as close as he thought prudent to observe them.

Dr. Doyle removed a pair of large tripods with an instrument attached to each one. Dr. Geaux carried another set. She headed to the east end of the island, while Dr. Doyle went west. This was his chance. It would be dangerous, and he must act quickly. With his boat engine in stealth mode, he approached the island from the south side. Carefully, he steered it parallel to the shore and navigated toward the west end, following Dr. Doyle.

After quickly anchoring the boat in shallow water, he waded onto the sand. Creeping through the underbrush, he moved silently into position behind Dr. Doyle, who knelt forty yards away, readying his instruments. The man was so intent on his work that he was oblivious to Dr. Catalyst's approach.

Dr. Catalyst aimed the tranquilizer rifle, sighting

down the barrel to a spot on Dr. Doyle's neck. He slowly let out his breath and pulled the trigger. Dr. Doyle stood up when the dart hit his neck, slapping at it, like a mosquito had bitten him. He stayed conscious long enough to remove the dart, staring at it without comprehension, then he sank to his knees and collapsed face-first on the ground.

Dr. Catalyst hurried forward as quietly as possible. Hefting the unconscious Dr. Doyle over his shoulders in a fireman's carry, he returned to his boat, laying him on the deck. Checking to make sure he was breathing and his pulse was steady, Dr. Catalyst leapt aboard, and with the silent engine engaged, the boat cut through the water.

When he was out of sight from the island he removed the goggles and engaged the main engine. The tablet on his console showed him the location of all the other NPS boats. It was a simple matter to avoid them on the way back to his compound. He knew the swamp far better than they did.

As he piloted the boat, he composed his next message to the media in his mind. *The park is to be closed, or Dr. Doyle shall perish.* The stubborn Dr. Geaux would have no choice but to do as he demanded.

Now the world would find out who was a charlatan and who was not.

20

AS THE BOYS CROSSED THE YARD, CALVIN BENDING Emmet's ear about Riley, Dr. Geaux emerged from the French doors onto the deck.

"Hello, boys," she said. "What are you up to?"

"Not a thing," Emmet said, hearing Calvin breathe a sigh of relief that the Riley discussion was at least temporarily over.

"I need you guys to come inside for a second," Dr. Geaux said.

Emmet wasn't sure why, but he felt a prickling sensation along the back of his neck.

"Where's my dad?" he asked as they entered the living room through the doors.

"Let's sit," Dr. Geaux said. Emmet could tell she was trying to stay calm, and that only made it worse.

"Where's my dad?" Emmet insisted.

Dr. Geaux sighed. "Emmet, I'm sure it's going to be okay, but right now your dad is missing."

Emmet's body tightened. It felt like electricity was crawling over his skin. This was the same feeling he'd experienced when his dad told him his mom was sick. And he didn't like it.

"What do you mean, 'missing'?!" Emmet shouted at Dr. Geaux.

Dr. Geaux took a deep breath. Emmet could see pain on her face, but right now he didn't care. She had brought Apollo with her from the office. His dad took him along to work every day, so he didn't have to stay home alone. The dog sensed Emmet's distress and stood on his hind legs, his forepaws on Emmet's waist. Emmet scooped him up in his arms and he licked Emmet's face and nose enthusiastically.

"He and I were setting up motion-sensor cameras on the island where those two things attacked you," she said.

"The pred-a-gators," Emmet said quietly.

"Yes, your father keeps calling them that now, too. As good a name as any, I guess. You remember when my rangers and I came back from the island? I carried a bag of . . . something?"

Emmet nodded, even though he barely remembered.

"When we searched the island, we found the fresh remains of a half-eaten python. It was literally torn in two. I brought a sample back and we tested it. We found DNA similar to that of the creature we have in the lab. Dr. Catalyst, as he calls himself, is definitely breeding these things to eat snakes. He needs the bird influence because some raptors can be trained to seek out a specific kind of prey," she said.

"What does this have to do with my dad?" Emmet asked.

"Ben . . . Dr. Doyle thought he might be using the island to test his creatures before he released them in the wild. It might have been a coincidence that you and Calvin just showed up on the island that day, but he thought it was worth investigating. Either way, Dr. Doyle thought we should set up motion-sensor cameras and we might get lucky and find out what he was up to." Dr. Geaux was obviously stressed and tired, but Emmet didn't care. He felt like yelling at her to get back out in the swamp and find his dad.

"Anyway," she went on, "he took his equipment to the west end of the island while I took the east end. This Dr. Catalyst keeps feeding the media and we've turned up no sign of him anywhere in the park. It was a shot in the dark, but there were no other leads. We thought we might catch a break."

"Where is he, Dr. Geaux? Where's my dad?" Emmet asked, his frustration mounting.

"Emmet, I'm sorry, but I don't know. Not right now. I came here to tell you. I've recalled every ranger I have to duty. First responders, county sheriffs, tour guides — anyone who has an airboat is out looking. I've got choppers, spotter planes, and the FBI is on the way with a tactical response team."

"How could he hide him? You must have some idea! You know that stupid swamp better than anyone!" Emmet insisted.

Dr. Geaux tried to stay calm.

"I think whoever this Dr. Catalyst is took your father hostage. We found a small tranquilizer dart on the ground by the cameras your dad was setting up. It's being tested now at the county crime lab, but I'm sure it will be some kind of paralyzing agent. This is good news. It means Dr. Catalyst took your father alive. But there are any one of a thousand places both in the swamp and out he could have taken him. But we will find your father. You have to believe me, Emmet."

"How is any of this good news? What does he want? Why my dad?" Emmet was doing everything he could to keep the tears from coming. To his surprise, Dr. Geaux took him in her arms and embraced both him and Apollo.

"Emmet, I don't know what he wants. I think your dad was a target of opportunity. The last few days Dr.

Catalyst has been saying he wants the park closed. I think this is his way of forcing our hand." She stood up again and put her hands on his shoulders.

"I've cleared it with the local police. I want you and Apollo to stay here with us until we find your dad. Which we are going to do, Emmet, I swear. I'm going to close the park. I'm going back to HQ in a few minutes and make the announcement to the news media."

"I'm going with you," Emmet said.

Dr. Geaux shook her head. "I don't think that's a good idea. I've got to coordinate —"

"I'm going!" Emmet said. "You can't keep —"

"Mom," Calvin interrupted quietly. "You can't close the park. You can't give him what he wants."

"What? Yes she can! If she closes the park, then he'll let my dad go," Emmet said.

Apollo started squirming, so Emmet set him down and Calvin got him a bowl of water.

"Every time you see the president or some police spokesman on television, they always say don't negotiate with terrorists, and —" Calvin started to say.

"Shut up, Calvin! Just shut up!" Emmet yelled.

He turned and sprinted back out the door and climbed up into the tree house. All he wanted was his dad back.

And he swore as soon as he saw him again they were getting in the truck and driving back to Montana.

21

DR. CATALYST FELT VICTORIOUS. DR. DOYLE REMAINED unconscious while he piloted the airboat to one of his secondary buildings. It was a fail-safe backup in case his original location was accidentally discovered. It was stocked with supplies and used an energy source similar to the one that powered his main compound. The past week was spent preparing it to hold a hostage. It was his original hope to capture one of Dr. Geaux's rangers, but he was overjoyed that his prize was Dr. Doyle, the eminent avian biologist.

Now everything was set. This would be his most dramatic broadcast yet, and he was certain it would send a tidal wave of fear through all of South Florida.

Dr. Geaux would have no choice. Her superiors would force her to close the Everglades.

Dr. Doyle was seated in a chair placed inside a heavy mesh-steel cage. His right arm was handcuffed to a steel chair bolted to the floor. A long length of chain was attached at the end of the cuff. The cage held the chair, a cot, and a small chemical toilet in one corner. There was a water cooler outside the cage, but within reach for his prisoner. The water was also mixed with a mild narcotic that would keep Dr. Doyle tired and less likely to think about escaping. In a cardboard box were several days' worth of protein bars. The cage was not tall enough for Dr. Doyle to stand up in, but he would be able to move around inside it. This would allow for Dr. Catalyst to leave him here alone, when he must attend to business elsewhere.

A web camera was affixed near the ceiling in a corner of the room. Another was attached to a steel bracket in front of the cage. He checked his laptop to make sure it was transmitting correctly. The split screen showed a close-up of Dr. Doyle, his eyes closed, his head drooped slightly forward.

The second screen was what would send shivers down the spine of anyone who watched it. It showed that Dr. Doyle's cage was placed atop a platform approximately two feet high. The floor around him was submerged in eighteen inches of water. The water contained some grasses and reeds Dr. Catalyst had removed from the swamp and placed inside the room. But it was what lurked beneath the water that was truly scary.

Swimming about the platform where Dr. Doyle sat unconscious were his two hybrids Hammer and Nails. Occasionally they lifted their elongated necks to peer around, and on the video screen the effect was chilling. Again, Dr. Catalyst had no intention of harming anyone if his demands were met. But if they were not, then he might be forced to take more drastic measures.

If Dr. Geaux did not close down the Everglades and allow him to release his hybrids to destroy the big snakes, he would open Dr. Doyle's cage and let Hammer and Nails inside. It would be another test of how his hybrids reacted when confronted with humans.

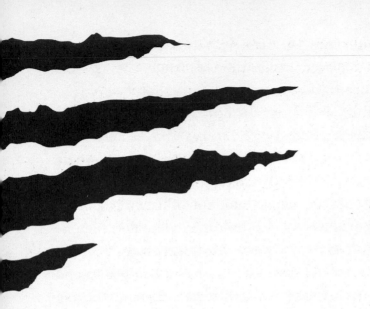

22

EMMET DIDN'T KNOW HOW LONG HE LAY ON THE TREE-house floor. Apollo circled the tree, barking and scratching at the trunk, whining for a while, until Emmet finally climbed down. Dr. Geaux was still in the house on her cell phone when he came back in. She and Calvin gave him some time and space, and he appreciated it. When he entered the kitchen she told whomever she was talking to that she would have to call back, and she stood up.

"I'm sorry, Emmet," she said again. "We're going to find your dad, I promise you."

"It's not your fault," Emmet said. "You didn't kidnap him. It's just . . ."

He couldn't go on. This didn't seem like the right time to talk about being afraid of losing his dad, just like he'd lost his mom. But Dr. Geaux understood.

"Emmet, I think I understand a little bit about what you're feeling right now. I've . . . we've . . . Calvin and I have lost someone, too. But my husband's death was an accident, and your mother was sick. Those are tragedies we couldn't do anything about. We can fight back here. And we're going to. We'll find him," she said.

She stood up and reached into her pocket, handing Calvin and Emmet cell phones. "I brought these over from the operations center. They're military-grade phones that we use in the park. I want both of you to keep these on you at all times. They've been pre-programmed with my number, the Florida City PD, Park Ranger Ops Center, Homestead PD, and the county sheriff's department. If you have any trouble, any trouble at all, you hit one or all of these buttons and you'll be surrounded by rangers and cops in a matter of minutes. There are chargers in the kitchen. Keep them fully charged at all times.

"Emmet," she said, looking at her watch. "It's about seven now. It's going to be dark soon. I was going to call my neighbor Mrs. Clawson to come stay with the two of you, but I've decided to take you both with me to park HQ. If your dad is in the swamp, I think he's going to want to see you when we find him. I'm going to be busy — and you're going to have to promise me you'll let us do our jobs — and in return I promise you we'll keep you informed. Deal?"

"All right," Emmet said.

Dr. Geaux smiled at him and put her hand on his head, running her hand through his hair. Emmet hadn't really thought about it before because she had an important job and was all business most of the time. But she was a mother, too. She understood what he was going through.

"Okay. Let's get Apollo and get back to HQ," she said.

The four of them piled into her silver Buick and hit the road.

23

UNBEKNOWNST TO EMMET, DR. CATALYST RELEASED the video feed of Dr. Doyle in captivity with the two hybrids in the water circling his cage. Within minutes it was running on every television channel and website in South Florida, and by the time they arrived, the media was in full-on insane mode. The main lot at the operations center was a mass of trucks and SUVs from every radio and TV station from Florida City to Miami.

Reporters with microphones chased after Dr. Geaux's car as it pulled up to the gate. Only a line of county sheriff's deputies kept the horde from surging through and following them all the way to the operations center. Still, they screamed and hollered questions at her through the car windows.

"Why are there so many reporters here?" Emmet asked.

"I told them I was holding a press conference at eight P.M., and everyone wants to get the best spot," she said. There was a falsely cheerful tone to her voice, and Emmet thought she wasn't telling him the whole truth. He wished he'd checked the TV before they left the house. It made him wonder if there was some new information about his dad she was keeping from him.

Calvin and Emmet, with Apollo in tow, went to wait in a conference room while Dr. Geaux stayed behind, speaking with a group of rangers, cops, and other law-enforcement personnel gathered in the parking lot. Inside, Calvin sat at the table while Emmet paced nervously back and forth across the floor. Apollo sat on his haunches watching Emmet for a while, then curled up in a ball and went to sleep.

"I'm sorry I yelled at you," Emmet said.

"No big deal," Calvin said, with the familiar shrug.

"You said there were protestors down here all the time. Has anything like this ever happened before?" Emmet asked. "Somebody being taken hostage or kidnapped?"

Calvin shook his head. "Not that I can remember. I don't recall Mom ever saying anything about it. Things can get heated, though. My mom . . . her job is not all that easy. She has to try to keep everyone happy, and gets pulled in a lot of different directions. You've got the environmental extremists, and those types who have all kinds of ideas about how the Everglades should be preserved. My mom says they range from 'the nutty to the reasonable.' At the other end you've got people who want to exploit the Everglades. They want to drain it all and build condos. Also nutty to reasonable. And then there're the people who want to open it wide to hunting, boating, all that. She gets a lot of grief from all of them." Calvin paused for a moment. "Even my dad."

"What do you mean?" Emmet asked.

"He was basically living out there when they met, in a camp. He was probably more on the 'close it down' or 'give it all back to the Seminoles and let them manage it' side of the 'what to do with the Everglades' debate. Right before my dad . . . at the end . . . they actually fought a lot about it," Calvin said.

"Really? It seems like they would be on the same side. My mom yelled at my dad sometimes, because he kind of has his head in the clouds a lot thinking about his work, but she was all about nature and supported my dad's career," Emmet said.

"Don't get me wrong," Calvin said. "They supported each other. I just think my dad was old-fashioned and my mom realizes that things are just too far gone, and someone has to make really hard choices to protect the River of Grass."

"River of Grass?" Emmet asked, confused.

"It's what the locals call the Glades sometimes," Calvin said.

Emmet couldn't stop pacing. He kept looking at the map of the park on the conference-room wall. It was an immense area, over one and a half million acres. He thought that if Dr. Catalyst was holding his father somewhere in the swamp, he could be anywhere.

"Calvin," Emmet asked. "Suppose you were going to kidnap someone and hide them in the Everglades. Where would you do it? Where would you stash them?"

"I wouldn't," Calvin said.

Emmet sighed. He'd only known Calvin for about a week, but he was beginning to suspect he was often intentionally difficult.

"I know you wouldn't kidnap someone. But let's just play 'pretend Calvin is a criminal.' Where would you hide someone if you did?" Emmet asked, trying and failing to keep the frustration out of his voice.

"No, I get what you're saying; what I mean is, I wouldn't keep anybody in the swamp," Calvin said.

"Why is that?" Emmet asked.

"Because there's nothing out there, except a few rustic cabins and that's it. And as big as it is, there're always rangers and tour guides and hunters and fishermen zipping by unexpectedly. Nope, if it were me, I'd hide them in a town, in a basement somewhere," Calvin said.

Emmet considered this while he paced.

"All right," Emmet said. "Another question. My dad told me whoever is making these predagators needs at least two things: a lot of knowledge about biology, and money. Just the computers and equipment to . . . I don't understand all of his scientist-speak, but he said something about 'creating the DNA models to properly construct recombinating genes' . . . or whatever . . . would cost tens, if not hundreds of thousands of dollars. So you'd require money and brains."

"I suppose," Calvin said.

Emmet stopped pacing.

"That's why whoever this is, whoever took my dad, has to be hiding in the Everglades!" he said.

Calvin frowned, and despite the seriousness of the moment, a small part of Emmet was glad it wasn't another shrug. He seemed to consider Emmet's point for a moment at least. Before he rejected it.

"Emmet, I know this is a lot of pressure, and it's a tense time, but —" Calvin was interrupted.

"You bet it is. And I'm going to find my dad somehow. But I'm not just saying this. Think about it," Emmet said.

"Think about what?" Calvin countered.

"This whole make-a-new-species thing. Whoever is doing this is smart and has money, or at least access to it. Maybe they stole it, who knows, it doesn't matter.

But like my dad said, they are inside a lab, running an experiment that is going back in time to the age of the dinosaurs. They're trying to re-create the itchy-actor-ox, or whatever my dad called it," Emmet said.

"Yes, and apparently they've succeeded, because we've seen them in action," Calvin said.

"Exactly! If you were this Dr. Catalyst, and you were spending who knows how much money and trying to re-create a species that lived a bajillion years ago, wouldn't you take every precaution? Wouldn't you make sure no one found out about it?" Emmet was getting excited.

"I . . . guess," Calvin said. He still seemed skeptical, and a little unsure of where Emmet was going.

"You would have to build your lab right in the swamp!" Emmet said. "Don't you see?"

"No. That would be the last place . . ." Calvin started to say, but Emmet waved him off.

"But one of his critters already escaped or died or something, because it's in your mom's dinosaur morgue, right?"

"Yes," Calvin said.

"There is no way somebody going to this much trouble would build their lab somewhere else, stir up some new species in a petri dish, hatch them, let them grow, and then bring them here to the swamp for a test drive. What if they got out? Or you were in a car accident on the way?

" 'What's that noise coming from your trunk, sir?' "
Emmet put his hands on his belt like a police officer
might. Then he pretended to be sitting at the wheel of
a car. " 'Oh, it's really nothing, Officer. Just some prehistoric creatures I cooked up in the basement of my
Homestead condo.'

"It would never work," Emmet went on. "And
nobody smart enough to do this would take that chance.
But if you were creating and testing those things here,
you'd be a lot less likely to be discovered. If one got
away, it might die and get eaten by something, or sink
to the bottom of the swamp. Or even if it was found,
like the one in the morgue, no one at the park is going
to say anything. They would do exactly what your
mom did. Keep the whole thing quiet to avoid a panic."
Emmet was getting more and more animated by the
minute.

"I'm not so sure," Calvin said. "And even if you're
right about the 'lab in the swamp' part, it doesn't mean
he's keeping your dad there."

"Just go with me for a minute. If this Dr. Caboose is
working alone, I don't think my dad would be kept too
far from his lab. He'd need to watch over his animals
and the hostage. And I don't think he'd keep them both
together, either, because he knows your mom is going
to move heaven and earth to find him. If they find my
dad *and* the lab, he's toast. Maybe they wouldn't be

right in the same place, but I bet they'd be close to each other," Emmet said.

"Dr. Caboose?" Calvin arched an eyebrow. "Do you always make up goofy names when you're nervous?"

"Yes. It's my thing. Like your shrug. But don't change the subject," Emmet said.

"Shrug? What shrug? I don't have a shrug," Calvin said. Of course, he shrugged while he said it.

"And that right there is what I'm talking about, but it's not important right now," Emmet said. "Where would you hide someone?"

"I don't . . ." Calvin hesitated. He walked over to stand in front of the map.

"Calvin, the first day we got here and went out in your boat, your mom said you were the best 'under eighteen' Everglades guide in Florida. Your boat is in tip-top shape; you do everything right according to that Manny guy on the radio. When the boat was disabled, you fixed it with some sand and spit. You have the world's biggest backpack and live in a tree house. . . ." Emmet said.

"I don't live there," Calvin insisted.

"And Riley likes you," Emmet said.

"No she doesn't!" Calvin said, his face starting to redden.

"See, you're getting mad. Try to think like Dr. Catalyst. You love the Everglades. It's being destroyed. You are going to save it. Taking this hostage will make them close the park and start to repair the damage. So where do you, Dr. Calvin, hide your hostage?"

Calvin sighed and gazed more intently at the map.

"There . . . it's just . . . there isn't much out there," Calvin started to say. "I don't see how it would work. You'd need power and there's hardly any way to get electricity out there."

"I thought you said your dad lived out there?" Emmet asked.

"He did. But it was a really rustic camp. No electricity or running water. He used batteries for light and propane to cook with. To do all the things you're saying, Emmet, it just doesn't seem possible," Calvin said.

"There's no electricity in the whole park?" Emmet asked.

"There is, just not a lot of it. The ranger stations have power, and a few of the public areas, to pump in freshwater, but . . ."

"What? But what . . . ?" Emmet said.

"Nothing."

"Calvin . . ." Emmet said. "If you've got an idea you better spill it. Or . . . or . . . so help me . . . you . . . My dad is missing and if you've got an idea that might save him you better start talking." Emmet stalked back and forth. He didn't know what else to do. Calvin was so deliberate in everything he did and Emmet was desperate. Then he thought of something.

"Speak. Or I'll call up Riley right now and tell her you don't like her and think she's weird."

Calvin's eyes got wide. "She is not weird, and you wouldn't . . ."

"Swear to God, I will, Calvin," Emmet said, pulling his cell phone out of his pocket. "I'll call her right now."

"All right . . . all right! *If* I was going to kidnap and hide somebody, there might be one place," Calvin said.

"Where?"

"Plantation Row. It's way on the far side of the park where hardly anyone goes anymore. It's where all the old, big sugarcane planters had mansions. Nobody has lived out there since the 1950s. But they must have used electricity back then, and it might be possible to get it turned on or use the existing power lines if you had the resources," Calvin said.

"Good," Emmet said, snapping the phone shut. "Take me there."

"What? I can't take you there. Are you insane? I would be in so much trouble. We'll tell the rangers and they'll . . ."

"Do you really think they're going to listen to me? I've seen search-and-rescue operations in the mountains in Montana. There are rules and grid searches and all kinds of —" He was interrupted by Dr. Geaux entering the office.

"I just wanted to check on you before I went to talk to the press," she said.

"Is there any news?" Emmet asked.

"No, I'm afraid not. But it's a big park and —"

"Mom," Calvin interrupted her, "Emmet has an idea about Dr. Catalyst that makes a lot of sense." Emmet stared at him, wondering why Calvin had changed his mind so suddenly.

"What is it, Emmet?" she asked.

"I . . . it's . . . I was just thinking, if I were . . ." he stammered at first, nervous and on edge, but then gave her a short version of his theory.

"I don't disagree. That makes a lot of sense. But I'm afraid Plantation Row has already been searched by the county sheriff's deputies. They didn't find anything." She tried to keep an upbeat expression on her face but failed. Emmet couldn't hide his disappointment. He shuffled across the office and slumped into the chair next to the desk.

"I'm sorry, Emmet," she said. "We're going to find him. You guys hang out here a little longer, and after my press conference we'll go home." She smiled as she left, but both of them could see the worry in her eyes.

"Dang it," Emmet said. Calvin didn't say anything

because he didn't know what to say. Instead, he picked up the remote for the TV on the wall, punched the on button, and set it on a local Miami station.

Emmet sat up straight in his chair and stared at the screen. They were expecting to see Dr. Geaux addressing the media. Instead, a very familiar face greeted them.

He was standing outside the park headquarters in front of a group of protestors holding signs. He spoke into a reporter's microphone and was wearing a green T-shirt that said SAVE THE EVERGLADES.

It was Dr. Newton.

24

DR. DOYLE CAME SLOWLY AWAKE. IT WAS A TOTAL
effort of mind and body just to move. It felt like
he'd been asleep for days. His arms and legs seemed
unreasonably heavy and it took every bit of strength
he possessed to lift his head from where it was hanging
limply against his chest. The smell of swamp water was
overpowering. He heard a splashing noise, and couldn't
process why he would hear water sounds indoors.
Maybe he *was* outside in the swamp.

He squinted with one eye, peering through the steel-
mesh cage, and was able to identify a cement wall.
He was definitely inside. But he couldn't understand
how his other senses would tell him he was also in the
swamp unless it was some sort of hallucination he was

experiencing. His eyes were reluctant to fully focus, but looking down, he found himself seated in a chair. His arm wasn't working correctly, and slowly he came to the realization that one of them was cuffed to the chair. But he didn't know why.

Remembering was difficult. He was somewhere in the Everglades doing something. Cameras. Setting up cameras. It was the last thing he could recall. There was no memory of how he arrived here. And now . . . he was . . . he had no idea.

Squinting, he tried to make his eyes work, closing one and then the other, but raising his head caused the room to spin wildly and he quickly closed them. All he knew was that he couldn't move yet and all he could think of was getting out of the chair and finding Emmet. He didn't want him to worry. But his legs and arms felt funny and he couldn't move. Why?

Slowly the fog curtain in his brain lifted. Now he could lift his head and glance around without growing dizzy. Why was he inside a cage? He must be drugged or sick, because he could not fathom how he arrived here. Certainly he wouldn't have climbed in and cuffed himself.

The chair he sat in was placed upon a wooden platform, and through the mesh he spied water and swamp grass. Had someone built a hut in the swamp and trapped him inside it?

There was a noise to his rear, something or someone splashing in the water. He could not move his head far enough to see what might be behind him.

"Who's there?" he mumbled, but his tongue was thick and his mouth didn't appear to be working correctly.

There was movement in the water to his left and now he was quite certain he was not alone. Something was inside the enclosure with him. Desperately he tried to clear his head, but whatever he'd been given was keeping him woozy. Fear trickled slowly into his mind.

Another splash sounded, this time right in front of him. Had he not been chained down, he would have jumped up and run away screaming. A reptilian head attached to a long birdlike neck popped out of the water. It stared at him with raptorlike eyes. He gasped in alarm, and at the noise the animal opened its mouth and hissed. All Dr. Doyle could focus on was row after row of sharp teeth.

As quickly as it was there it was gone, darting below the surface. He shook his head back and forth, noticing the water cooler. His tongue was thick and he was thirsty. Bent over at the waist, he clambered on unsteady legs to the faucet. Turning the spigot, he cupped the water into his hand and gulped down several mouthfuls. It gave only temporary relief and he drank more. Slumping back into the chair, he tried to think, but a few minutes later, a sleepy feeling overcame him, and though he tried fighting it, his eyes closed and could not be forced open.

His head bobbed forward again, chin landing on his chest. Just as his head sank, the creature launched itself out of the water, gliding through the air. Its long claws raked across the steel mesh before latching onto the cage. It unleashed a low-throated bugling call and another creature answered its cry. Large jaws snapped closed as its eyes focused on Dr. Doyle inside the cage.

Dr. Doyle would have no doubt screamed in fear at the abrupt appearance of the creature. But he was already unconscious.

25

"WE OBVIOUSLY DON'T BELIEVE IN TAKING HOSTAGES,"
Dr. Newton said. "And we think these hybrid
creatures this 'Dr. Catalyst' has apparently bred
need more study. But the sad fact is, as he indicates,
pythons and boa constrictors are destroying the
Everglades' ecosystem. If he has a viable option for
restoring the balance of nature, then he should have a
seat at the table."

Emmet was stunned. Calvin wore a calm, thoughtful
expression on his face, as usual. Except for his eyes.
There was something in his eyes. Emmet wasn't quite
sure what it was, but it wasn't shock or outrage. He
knew that.

"You've got to be kidding me! What is that jack wagon doing on television? And don't you dare shrug. He's on Dr. Catalyst's side? I don't believe it!" Emmet was almost shouting.

The TV report cut back to the studio and Calvin turned off the set.

Emmet launched himself out of his chair and was really pacing back and forth now.

"He's actually *supporting* this kidnapper?" he stormed.

Calvin looked really uncomfortable. "I'm sorry you saw that. It's like I told you, there are all kinds of people down here that believe a bunch of crazy things," he said calmly.

"There's crazy and there's *crazy*! Somebody. Kidnapped. My. Dad. Does no one understand that?"

Emmet's rant woke Apollo from his slumber and he sat up, watching as Emmet paced around the conference room. The dog whined and Calvin sat on the floor next to him and scratched his ears, for which he received a thorough face-washing in appreciation. Calvin didn't complain, so Apollo flipped over on his back, waiting for the belly rub he thought he deserved. Calvin complied.

Emmet couldn't remember ever being this angry. So mad that words failed him. It was bad enough some crackpot had taken his dad hostage. Now he had to see people out there who were on said crackpot's side.

He snatched the remote control off the desk and switched the TV back on. This time, Dr. Geaux was answering questions from reporters.

"Will the park close?" came a question from a blond lady with a microphone.

"In accordance with policies already in place, the park will be closed to civilian visitors until we locate Dr. Doyle. This will allow all search efforts to be coordinated and free from interference of non-search personnel," Dr. Geaux said. She was using her formal "don't mess with me because I'm the park superintendent" voice.

"Have you received any direct contact from the suspect calling himself Dr. Catalyst?" another reporter shouted.

"We have not been directly contacted by anyone claiming to be the criminal suspect in this case," Dr. Geaux said.

"Dr. Geaux!" another man with headphones and a microphone shouted at her. "I'm sure you are aware of the protests taking place right outside the park. Some environmental groups are actually portraying Dr. Catalyst as a hero. Do you have any comment on that?"

Dr. Geaux's face reddened. Even on television, Emmet could tell it was an all-out struggle for her not to reach out and strangle the reporter with her bare hands. She took a second to compose herself before answering.

"The last time I checked, 'heroes' don't kidnap innocent victims to advance their agendas," Dr. Geaux said. "That's all the time I have for questions. Anything further will be handled by the park media relations staff." She turned on her heel and walked through the gate with her head up and shoulders straight. A woman of purpose. If he hadn't been so frantically worried, Emmet would have congratulated her for her demeanor when she walked into the room a few minutes later.

She glanced at the TV, which was already replaying her response to the last question of her press conference. Then she looked at Emmet.

"I'm sorry you saw that," she said.

"It's okay. You did good. I would have given that guy a 'bow to the dome,' " Emmet said.

Dr. Geaux and Calvin looked confused.

"Sorry. Snowboarder slang. An elbow to the face," Emmet said.

She smiled and sat down at the table, rubbing her eyes and trying to stifle a yawn.

"Emmet," she said. "I'm sorry, but it's dark, and we're going to have to recall the boats until first light. Even with spotlights, it's too dangerous to have watercraft zipping around in the dark. There are stumps, floating logs, any number of ways for accidents to happen. We're going to keep choppers up with infrared, and my rangers and local police will keep watching the roadways, although I don't expect the road patrols to find anything. The choppers might, though."

Emmet's heart sank, unable to bear the thought of his father being out there even a second longer. Try as he might, he couldn't think of an argument to counter what Dr. Geaux said. The last thing his dad would want would be for someone to get hurt while they were looking for him. He tried telling himself that his dad was a strong guy who'd spent a lot of time in the wilderness. And if he was being held hostage, he was probably someplace at least temporarily safe. None of these thoughts made him feel any better.

He looked at Dr. Geaux, his face in anguish. There was something he wanted to say, but he couldn't get it out. Surprisingly, Calvin came to his rescue again. He was turning into a regular public speaker, that Calvin.

"Mom, Emmet has something else to ask," Calvin blurted out. Emmet was glad he'd said it, but not sure if Dr. Geaux was in a mood to hear any more of their theories.

"What's that?" she asked.

"I just wondered if you thought there might be any way Dr. Newton could be involved," Emmet said.

Dr. Geaux's exhaustion was showing clearly on her face, and Emmet thought she might find his idea ludicrous. But this time she surprised him. Instead of discounting what he said, she sat back in her chair for a moment and steepled her hands in front of her, eyebrows knitted, and stared up at the ceiling for a few seconds. The silence made it nearly unbearable for Emmet.

Finally she said, "You know, I hadn't thought about him. What I mean is, I know he's out there protesting, but I didn't think about it from the angle that he might be involved." She was quiet a minute longer.

"Calvin told me he comes from money and he's always harping about everyone ruining the Everglades," Emmet said. "My dad said whoever was creating these creatures would have to have a lot of financing just for the equipment. They'd also have to know a lot about biology, and he's a doctor. So . . ." Emmet let the thought hang there.

"Hmm," Dr. Geaux said. "I have to tell you, I've had a long and often tempestuous association with Dr. Newton. I think his heart is in the right place, but sometimes his . . . personality . . . gets in the way. And he does have money. He's always donating it to causes and groups here. But I have to be honest with you, I don't see him going this far."

"But . . ." Emmet started to protest, but Dr. Geaux held up her hand to stop him.

"Still, the Everglades is a federal facility, so I'm going to get an FBI agent I've dealt with before to interview him. Steve has a sixth sense about these things. If Dr.

Newton is involved, my money is on Steve worming it out of him. Does that sound fair?"

Emmet agreed that it did.

"All right," Dr. Geaux said. "It's time to go home. Emmet, we can swing by your house and get what you need for a few days, and some food for Apollo. Then I want you both in school tomorrow. There really isn't anything you can do here. And I promise if we find your dad, we'll bring him straight to you."

At the mention of "food" and "Apollo," the little black mutt sat up on his hind legs and vocalized his opinion. It was immediately understood by all of them that both words shouldn't be used in the same sentence unless the food was readily available.

Emmet didn't like feeling so helpless. He wanted to go grab Dr. Newton himself and throw him in a room and find out what he knew. But he couldn't do that. He had to go home with Dr. Geaux. Go to school and pretend nothing happened.

And he did a pretty good job of it. Right up until he couldn't take it anymore.

26

AFTER THEY'D PICKED UP HIS CLOTHES AND APOLLO'S food and returned to the Geauxs' home, Emmet switched on his laptop. The video of his dad was everywhere. He nearly lost it. He realized Dr. Geaux was trying to protect him, but he was still mad. With the laptop in his hand, he stormed into the kitchen and interrupted Dr. Geaux and Calvin, who were talking at the counter.

"I don't blame you, Emmet," she said, when he confronted her. Her voice sounded full of remorse. "I was trying to spare you and I was wrong. I should have let you know. There are several websites running the feed continuously, but Dr. Catalyst clearly knows his way around a computer. We can't trace the transmission back to the source."

Emmet tried not to let his disappointment show. Dr. Geaux was exhausted, and he knew she had been working nonstop since his dad had been taken earlier that day. "I know you're worried, Emmet."

"I wish you'd stop saying that," Emmet muttered. He looked at the suitcase in the hallway.

"Emmet, come with me, please," she said. They left Calvin in the kitchen, cleaning. He was rubbing the same spot on the counter with a damp rag and trying to look useful. They stepped through the French doors into the backyard. It was cooler now, and completely dark out.

There was a redwood bench underneath one of the cypress trees and she motioned for Emmet to sit next to her. She leaned back against the tree, still in uniform; her boots and pants were splattered with mud. Her sidearm was attached to her belt. Before his dad disappeared that morning, he'd never seen her wear it.

"Emmet, I like you. And I like and respect your father. He's really quite a brilliant man. And I feel responsible that he . . . that you both were caught up in this. But when I asked every agency in the government for the best avian biologist out there, his was the only name that came back. When we found that first hybrid, and the test results came back . . ." She stopped and massaged her shoulders with her hands.

"Then you and Calvin met up with those creatures on the island that day. When we went back there and found the partially eaten python . . . it all sort of slipped into place. I didn't know everything, but I had an idea then what someone was trying to do. That what we'd found wasn't some new mutated or transplanted species. Someone was playing with nature. And it had the potential to be very bad. Now it is. I can't change that. The only thing I can do is find your dad. And I will. I swear to you," she said.

"But I do know how you're feeling, Emmet. When Calvin's dad . . . my husband . . . disappeared . . . I —"

Emmet interrupted her, "What do you mean 'disappeared'? I thought you said he died in an accident?"

She looked up at the dark sky. Emmet realized it was painful for her to talk about. But he was also angry, no matter how bad he felt about it. Once, his dad took him fly-fishing on the Yellowstone River. After his first couple of casts, his line was hopelessly tangled into an orange-sized knot. He'd thought his dad would be angry, but he just laughed until they were both laughing.

He felt like that knot. Like if his dad didn't come back he'd never get untied. And it felt even worse because he couldn't do anything about it.

"No, officially he was declared dead. His airboat crashed on a night hunt. It caught fire and spun into a hillock and collided with a mangrove tree. Knowing Lucas, he tried to save the stupid boat, and may have been burned or overcome by heat and smoke. They dragged the area around the crash site but couldn't find his body.

"We waited weeks for news," she went on. "It was worse not knowing. It's changed Calvin. But the thing is, Lucas loved the Everglades. I think Calvin probably told you his father was a Seminole. If he was going to die, he would have wanted to be returned to his beloved swamp. That made finally accepting it a little easier."

Emmet was quiet, his head down. He felt Dr. Geaux's hand fall gently on the back of his neck. It was comforting, in a way.

"But like I said, Lucas's death was an accident. Your father is still alive and we are going to find him, Emmet. I know I keep swearing to you, but it doesn't make it less true. And when I say I know a little about how you feel, I do. And so does Calvin. Even if he doesn't always know how to show it."

Emmet felt like there was nothing else to say. He was worn out. And he believed Dr. Geaux was telling the truth. They were doing everything they could to find his dad.

But he needed to do something. If he didn't, he was never going to untangle the knot inside him.

27

DR. CATALYST WAS SO EXCITED HE COULD BARELY CHOOSE which monitor to watch. His video updates were being replayed constantly on local and even national networks. Websites sprang up declaring him both a hero and a villain. He paid no attention to the latter. Most agents of change, most "catalysts" that brought forth new ideas and challenges to the accepted order, were considered both heroic and villainous.

He kept careful watch over Dr. Doyle. There were a few close calls with patrols nearly discovering where he'd hidden the good doctor, but so far he'd avoided detection. The helicopters worried him at first, but he so carefully guarded his compounds against infrared detection that a few passes by the choppers without discovery left him unworried.

He constantly monitored his captive, making sure the water cooler was still full of the mildly drugged water, just enough to keep Dr. Doyle in a state of constant slumber. Soon he would need to return to the compound to feed his Pterogators, but he felt Dr. Geaux would cancel the search for the night. Unable to find Dr. Doyle, she would have to give in to his demand to close the park permanently. Then his Pterogators could go to work restoring the balance of nature.

If Dr. Doyle were somehow rescued, Dr. Catalyst would almost certainly lose Hammer and Nails. He needed them in place as de facto sentries in case Dr. Doyle did wake up. Losing his first hybrid was painful, but Hammer and Nails were his first successful pair, and they were special. They had proven to be exactly what he envisioned. And now their "offspring" were nearly ready to follow their lead.

He called them offspring, even though this new batch of hatchlings were technically clones. Given how rapidly the snakes destroyed the ecosystem, he made certain his hybrids could not reproduce. They would not overrun the swamp this way. It was why he was so desperate to get his hands on the corpse in Dr. Geaux's lab. To run his own tests, and find out what happened to the creature. It was most certainly an accidental death, but even a brilliant scientist such as himself could not assume anything. But getting the corpse back would have to wait.

On another monitor, the image showed half a dozen hybrids in the final stages of devouring a python inside the main tank in his lab. If anything, they were proving more voracious than Hammer and Nails. Given the choice between snake and other prey, they chose snake every time. His gene sequencing and hormone therapy worked perfectly. He'd created the ultimate apex predator the Everglades so sorely needed. One that would not threaten the native crocodilians, but would eventually destroy the invasive snakes.

The enormity of what he accomplished washed over him like a wave. No other scientist had ever accomplished this. The creation of an entirely new species. One whose birth would save his beloved River of Grass.

Dr. Geaux finally gave in. She closed the park. Now all he needed to do was wait for her to agree to his demand to keep the park closed permanently and end the search. No matter how she persisted, soon the time and resources of the local agencies would wane. Dr. Geaux would always keep looking, but the police and FBI would have to turn to other duties. He would only release Dr. Doyle when he was given assurances that the park would remain closed forever to the outside world.

There was still much work to do. Another group of hatchlings was needed to make certain his creations survived the rigors of the swamp. All in good time. Right now, he was going to take a moment and revel in his unparalleled success.

28

I N A STRANGE WAY, DR. NEWTON HAD A LOT TO DO WITH Emmet's plan to find his father. Emmet started yelling at Dr. Newton the minute he walked into the school the next morning. Yelling so loud that Calvin felt the need to get between him and the teacher. Given Emmet's feelings and the tension of the situation, Dr. Newton felt it would be best that Emmet be moved to another science class. Ms. Susskind became his science teacher.

She was teaching a unit on the circulatory system of the human body. They looked at slides and studies comparing cold-blooded and warm-blooded species. His schedule was rearranged when he was moved from Dr. Newton's class, and science was his first class of the day. The lesson gave him an idea. He thought about it all through the day.

At lunch, he sat at the table with everyone as usual. While they carried on their normal conversations, Emmet stared off into space. His brain felt like a giant jigsaw puzzle that was missing the one final piece. It was like the idea he needed, the one thing that might help find his dad, was yet to slip into its proper place.

"Emmet, I know you've been asked this enough times you probably want to scream but . . . are you all right?" Raeburn asked.

"Huh . . . what?" Emmet snapped out of his reverie.

"She wanted to know if you are feeling okay," Riley said.

"Yes, I feel fine. Why?"

"You just seem a little distracted, is all," Raeburn said.

"Distracted? No. I don't think so," Emmet said.

"Really? Because you just ate Stuke's sandwich," Calvin said.

"I did no —" He looked down to see his sandwich still on his tray while Stuke's tray was sandwich-free. Stuke was sitting there, too polite to mention anything, but looking hungry all the same.

"Oh. Dude, I am so sorry, I . . . Here, take mine," Emmet offered.

"It's really okay," Stuke said.

"Please, Stuke. I guess I just wasn't paying attention. Seriously, take it."

Stuke gratefully took the sandwich. "I don't suppose there's any news," he asked Emmet.

"No."

"Well, my dad says they're turning the swamp upside down," Stuke said.

"I know," Emmet said quietly. "Everybody is doing their best. Listen, I'm sorry, but I've got to go."

"Where?" Calvin asked.

"Just the library," Emmet said. He excused himself from the table, and as he was leaving, heard Riley and Raeburn chastising Stuke. Stuke kept saying "What'd I do?" repeatedly. Emmet knew the poor guy didn't mean any harm, but he still didn't want to talk about it. He needed to *do* something about it. If he went another minute without somehow helping to find his dad, he might just go crazy.

He had told a white lie to his friends. Emmet didn't go to the library but instead headed to the school office. At lunchtime he knew it would be mostly empty, except for Mrs. Connors, the office manager; and probably Double J, who had been sent for another visit with the principal, Mr. Wallace.

"Hi there, Emmet!" she said when he walked in. Mrs. Connors was always cheerful.

"Hey, Mrs. Connors," Emmet said. He held up his phone. "It's almost time for me to call Dr. Geaux. Is it okay if I use the conference room?"

"Of course," she said. "You go right ahead and just holler if you need anything."

He went inside the conference room and shut the door. The phones he and Calvin were given had web browsers. The media had finally stopped running Dr. Catalyst's constant feed showing Dr. Doyle in the metal cage. A few rogue sites out there were showing it, but the authorities were making them take down the feeds whenever they popped up. Emmet didn't understand why people would want to show something so horrible, and he resisted the urge to look for one. He didn't want to see his dad like that. Once was enough.

Emmet was looking for information. The science class had gotten him thinking. About heat and cold and alligators and the swamp and the infrared detectors Dr. Geaux had said were being used to search for his dad. And how all the animals were migrating out of the park, so there should be no residual heat signatures from them. And how there might be one small chance that Dr. Catalyst overlooked something in his little plan.

One small chance.

All Emmet needed was a certain piece of information, but he wasn't sure how he was going to get it. If he started asking strange questions, Dr. Geaux or Calvin were almost certain to pick up on it. In the end, he knew he was going to have to be sneaky. The thought of deceiving Dr. Geaux made him feel uncomfortable, but he couldn't see any other way around it. It was his theory, and he wasn't going to tell anyone who might not take it seriously. His dad was now missing for over twenty-four hours.

The previous night, Dr. Geaux had walked in with a briefcase full of reports and printouts. After she and Emmet talked in the yard, she'd sent them on to bed and went to her den to work. She was gone before they woke for school. The neighbor, Mrs. Clawson, came by to check on them and make sure they got on the bus. Mrs. Clawson was also going to check in on Apollo during the day.

After school, Emmet and Calvin came home and played with the pooch in the yard and took him for a walk before doing homework in the tree house. Emmet admitted he was growing very fond of Calvin's tree house. It was a small thing, only a few feet up in a tree, but somehow the world looked different from up here. And with each step up the side of the tree, it was like his problems stayed below on the ground.

When Dr. Geaux came home that night, she was near complete exhaustion. The park remained closed to visitors, so it allowed her to deploy all of her personnel toward the search. But it was taking a toll on her, too.

"Good evening, boys," she said. Apollo rushed to greet her, just like he did to anyone who came to the door. Any visitor was an explosion of barking and tail wagging. Dr. Geaux knelt down and let Apollo clean the worry off her face. It never failed to get a laugh out of her. Emmet's feelings were all mixed up, and part of him was still mad at Dr. Geaux for getting his dad involved in this in the first place. But he had to admit she was a nice person.

Mrs. Clawson left them a Crock-Pot with beef stew and biscuits to warm up for dinner, and the three of them ate in relative silence. When they were finished, Calvin and Emmet did the dishes while Dr. Geaux went to her study. She came out a few minutes later. They avoided talking about the search for Emmet's dad. It just hung there like a giant black cloud. So far, they weren't able to find him.

"Guys," she said. "I'm beat. I'm going to sleep. I'll see you tomorrow."

After that, Emmet waited. And waited. Every once in a while, up in Montana, the snowfall came softly . . . the snow falling out of the sky in big puffy flakes that seemed to take hours before they landed on the ground. For Emmet, the minutes went by like one of those snowflakes. Each one taking its own sweet time to pass. He was so tense it felt like whatever he did was giving away everything. Even when he tried to act as normal as possible, he worried that Calvin would think he was acting too normal and would sniff out his plan.

Finally, Calvin went to bed, and Emmet followed along. Just like the night before. He brushed his teeth and got ready to go to sleep. But he wouldn't be sleeping tonight. From his spot in the guest room he stayed awake for a few more hours, reading, getting up and pacing the floor when he felt sleepy. All night long he kept it up, until it was almost four A.M.

He opened the guest-room door, checking to see that Calvin's and Dr. Geaux's doors were still shut. Apollo looked up at him from his bed on the floor, but it was his sleep time and he dropped his head back down, not at all interested in what Emmet was up to.

Still in his clothes, he crept downstairs to Dr. Geaux's study. Her briefcase was open on the desk, a bunch of file folders inside it. Emmet flipped on the small desk lamp and looked through the files until he found the one he wanted. He pulled the map out of the file and spread it open on her desk, studying it carefully. Fifteen minutes later, he was pretty sure he found what he was looking for.

Emmet took the file with him and quietly and cautiously crept to the front door. Hoping for no squeak or whining hinges, he carefully opened it. Then he slipped away into the darkness.

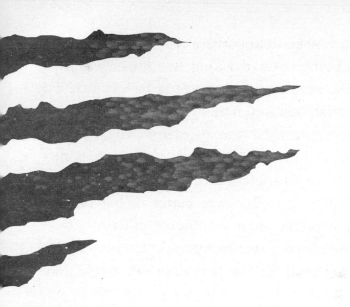

29

THE FLORIDA CITY BUSES RAN THROUGH THE NIGHT.
Though he had only been in town for a week, Emmet
studied the routes on a map at school and knew the bus
that would drop him off within walking distance of
the park. He wasn't sure exactly how he'd get inside.
But he'd come this far. The rest of it . . . he would just
have to figure it out when he got there.

On their first day in Florida, when Emmet and his
dad followed Dr. Geaux to the park, she drove them
through a separate entrance, about a mile away from
the main gate. There lay the facility storing the dead
archosaur, and behind it, the path that led to the docks.
That was Emmet's destination. He didn't want to run
into any media, protestors, or other commotion at the

main entrance, even though there was likely to be little going on this early in the morning. Besides, he was willing to bet Dr. Geaux's entrance would be less guarded and easier to talk his way into.

When he approached the gate from the road he couldn't believe his luck. There was nobody stationed there. You needed a special card to raise the gate. Dr. Geaux probably figured it was better to put rangers out on search parties than keeping them back here at the gate, where no one was likely to get in, anyway. He started to feel good for the first time in a while, like maybe this was going to work.

As he walked closer to the entrance, the realization that he hadn't thought this all the way through smacked him in the head. The gate was at least ten feet high, and the surface was smooth. The walls rose up on either side of the gate, making them taller yet; at least twelve feet high. But he had come this far, and he wasn't going to give up easily.

Emmet was about five and a half feet tall. He wouldn't be able to jump and reach the top. He tried not to let the sense of dejection take over, but it was hard not to. Then he spotted the trash can a few yards down the road. If he used it like a makeshift stepladder . . . it would still leave him a little short from the top . . . but it might give him just enough lift to reach the top. A few weeks ago he'd been snowboarding in Montana and his legs were still in pretty good shape. If he took a running start and used the can as a launching pad, he could probably grab the top and scramble over.

Probably.

He retrieved the trash can and turned it upside down up against the gate. If someone came along and saw it there, he hoped they wouldn't put two and two together. Maybe they'd think the wind blew it off the road.

Emmet backed up and took a deep breath. He ran as hard as he could toward the trash can, then jumped up and pushed off against the bottom of it. For a moment, it looked like it was going to work. Until all of a sudden the gate was swinging open while he was still in midair.

Emmet had planned for almost everything. Just not Calvin.

30

THEY ENDED UP NOT TAKING THE *DRAGONFLY 1.* CALVIN chose a canoe instead, one with an electric trolling motor that was almost silent.

"Probably better to give up a little speed for noise," he'd said when he'd finally agreed to Emmet's plan. Now Emmet wasn't so sure. The canoe was way slower than the airboat. But Calvin swore it was the right choice, and so they got in and off they went. Calvin made sure the battery was fully charged, and he even removed two spares from two of the other boats in case they needed them. Emmet was pretty sure Calvin thought over everything. He'd also brought Apollo along on his leash.

A breeze was coming out of the west, and suddenly Emmet remembered Dr. Geaux telling him she must bring the boats back from the search efforts at night. It was too dangerous to be zipping around in an airboat in the dark, she'd said. Too many stumps and floating logs and other obstacles to collide with if you couldn't see where you were going. The canoe was slower, sure. But Emmet was holding on extra tight. The morning light was brightening by the moment, but he was hoping like heck they didn't crash headlong into a stump. He was pretty sure Calvin knew the swamp like Apollo knew pork chops, and could pilot a boat through blindfolded if necessary. He still held on, though.

It took some convincing. As sure as Emmet was that Dr. Catalyst was running his entire operation out of the swamp, Calvin was equally convinced he wasn't. But to Calvin's credit, he'd listened to Emmet's theory — really listened. Of course then he tried to poke holes in it. They discussed it back and forth by the gate, Emmet still aching from his crash into it.

Calvin, with Apollo acting like a bloodhound, had followed him the whole way. Just as Emmet jumped, he used his mom's card on the reader by the street to open the gate. Instead of grasping the top and climbing over, Emmet crashed into it with a *thud*. Calvin thought it was funny. What a comedian.

Emmet confessed that his plan was to take the *Dragonfly 1* out into the swamp to search, which sounded foolish in retrospect. Besides, he didn't know how to pilot a boat, and he'd made one other pivotal mistake.

"If you're going to pilot an airboat, you need to know at least one thing," Calvin said while they stood there, Emmet growing more nervous by the minute that someone would come along and spot them.

"What's that?" Emmet said.

Calvin reached into his pocket and removed a key chain. "Where the keys are."

Emmet groaned. He hadn't even thought of that. The day they went out in the boat he never paid attention to how it started. Maybe by pushing a button. It was a freaking boat, not a car.

Emmet thought Calvin would turn him in, then. He'd have to go to Dr. Geaux and apologize for taking the documents he needed from her briefcase, tell them why, and wait while the giant bureaucracy considered his idea. In the meantime his dad would still be out there. Finally, he'd won Calvin over by asking him a question.

"Calvin, if you were in my spot, if it was your mom out there, what would you do?"

Calvin had considered it a moment, but not a long one. Then he said, "Let's go. But we're not taking the *Dragonfly One*."

Now they were almost to the first coordinates on the map Calvin had taken from Dr. Geaux's study that evening. Emmet had shown Calvin the spot and he'd put the coordinates into the GPS unit he pulled from his backpack. It took them nearly an hour to get there. The first place Emmet thought Dr. Catalyst might be hiding his dad was a location about a mile deep in the swamp, but close to Plantation Row. Except for one problem.

There was nothing there.

A hillock of dry ground rose up out of the surrounding water, but it was covered in saw grass and shrubs and other bushes Emmet couldn't identify. He had been so sure. Now he just felt like an idiot, and even worse, he thought his dad . . . No. No matter what, he would not allow himself to think it.

"There's nothing here," Emmet said bitterly.

"Look," Calvin said suddenly, standing up and pointing to the . . . Emmet had no idea what he was pointing at.

"At what?" Emmet said.

"There's something not right about those tufts of grass in the middle . . . of . . . They're higher . . . Wait here," he said. Using a boat hook, he grabbed a small sapling and pulled them close enough to the hillock for him to step out onto it. He crashed through the grass and stopped. Calvin took Apollo, still on his leash, with him. Emmet waited in the boat, feeling a little scared and a bit ashamed. His dad was missing and he should be helping Calvin search. But the swamp still scared him.

"Emmet! Come here," Calvin said.

Emmet took a deep breath and stepped out of the canoe. He followed their path through the grass until they were standing next to each other. Calvin was still holding the boat hook. But Apollo was moving back and forth, sniffing the ground like crazy and digging at the grass and roots.

"What?" Emmet said.

Calvin poked the boat hook into the ground. There should have been either a loud squishing sound or no sound at all. Instead it made a thunking sound.

"It's concrete," Emmet said.

"Yep, and there's got to be a way inside. Look around for a hatch or door," Calvin said.

They stomped around, pushing the grass back and forth. Emmet was nearly ready to give up when Apollo barked. Now the little mutt was digging furiously at the ground with his paws. Calvin yelled, "Over here!"

Apollo uncovered a small electrical switch box. Opening the cover revealed a red-and-green button on a small panel inside.

"Push it," Emmet said.

"What if it's a tr —" Calvin didn't get a chance to finish, because Emmet reached over and pushed the button. They heard a whirring sound like a motor, and six feet in front of them a hatch covered in grass and weeds slowly flipped open, revealing a damp, musty stairway leading down into darkness.

Calvin looked at Emmet.

"You first," he said.

31

THE KLAXON SOUND OF A PERIMETER ALARM WOKE DR.
Catalyst from sleep. He came awake instantly, but
was not immediately concerned. It was probably a deer
or an alligator that had activated one of the motion
sensors he placed around all of his compounds. It had
happened plenty of times before. But when he ambled
over to the monitor, still rubbing the sleep from his
eyes, his heart nearly leapt from his chest.

The alarm was tripped from the holding bunker
where he kept Dr. Doyle. He'd installed wireless
cameras to cover the area, and he pulled up a screen
of images. What he saw made him feel weak. A canoe
bobbed gently in the water next to the hillock where
the bunker was built. Someone found it? Impossible.

His mind raced. How could this have happened? Had Doyle come awake and somehow summoned help? This couldn't be! It must have been a ranger who had stumbled across the bunker by blind luck. He was too careful. It was so well hidden.

There was simply no time for self-recrimination. The bunker was now compromised, and it would soon be crawling with law enforcement. He took a deep breath to calm himself. This was unexpected and unfortunate, but nothing he hadn't planned for.

Furiously, he began implementing his evacuation. He could load his new round of hatchlings onto the boat, and the latest batch of eggs in the battery-powered incubator. He'd trained and rehearsed for this eventuality many times. *Stick to the plan*, he reminded himself. *Calm is slow, slow is fast*: a mantra he repeated to himself in tense situations.

As he slipped into his jumpsuit, his eye caught the monitor again and he studied the boat more closely. It suddenly occurred to him that it was a canoe and not an airboat. Park rangers would not be using canoes; they were too slow. And if it wasn't a park-service craft, whose could it be? One of the volunteer guides or . . . no . . . a poacher looking for gators?

Just then, Calvin and the Doyle boy emerged from the stairway, and it appeared they were arguing over something. From their body language and gestures, he deduced that Calvin was trying to convince the Doyle lad to refrain from descending the stairs. He threw back his head and laughed.

"Good advice, Calvin!" he shouted to the empty room. "He doesn't have any idea what is waiting for him down there!"

He watched a few more seconds as the Doyle boy held the leash of a small black dog and stayed by the entrance as Calvin retreated to the canoe. He returned with a large black Maglite and a first-aid kit.

These two were clever. Maybe his plan to save the Everglades wasn't going to go as smoothly as he thought. If they entered and somehow got past Hammer and Nails and saved Dr. Doyle, there was a chance his creations could escape. If they left the door open, Hammer and Nails might leave the bunker in search of snakes.

Dr. Catalyst had not fitted them with their collars while they were inside the bunker. If they got away, he might not recover them. While he planned to release more of his hybrids to clear out the snake population, it was always his intention to do so in a carefully calculated way. He wanted to make sure they were monitored. Both for their own health and safety, and to document the decline of the snake population.

Dr. Catalyst felt a strange feeling flowing over him. At first he only intended to hold Dr. Doyle hostage as a means to an end. He did not intend to harm the man.

But now these two precocious boys were on the verge of undoing everything he'd devoted years to. Could he seriously allow that?

He looked at the clock. It was 5:30 A.M. The search patrols would be starting in another hour or so. There wasn't much time. What was he prepared to do? Come this close and lose? For several seconds he sat stock-still, considering his options.

Then he came to a decision. Slipping on the hood that concealed his face, he grabbed the keys and raced to his airboat. Calvin and Emmet gave him no choice. It wasn't his fault. As difficult as it might be for some to grasp, individuals were not as important as the preservation of nature.

He would have to destroy them all.

32

EMMET WAS THREE STEPS DOWN THE STAIRS WHEN HE felt Calvin's hand on his collar pulling him back up. He jerked and tried to break loose, not understanding what Calvin was doing. It was too dark to see much, but he definitely heard something moving in the darkness below.

"What? What are you doing? My dad is down there," Emmet nearly shouted.

"We don't know that for sure," Calvin said calmly. "But if he is, Emmet, you've seen the broadcast and you know what's down there with him. Wait here." Calvin trotted back in the direction of the boat.

"Where are you going?" Emmet shouted. He looked

down into the darkened bunker again, because he thought he'd heard a splash when he shouted.

Calvin was back right away. He was carrying a big Maglite flashlight, which he handed to Emmet. He kept the boat hook and was now holding a first-aid kit. Emmet switched on the light and shined it down the stairway. He saw water at the bottom of the steps, and it only made him quicken his pace down the stairs. Calvin stayed one step behind him. The water was filled with grass from the swamp, but it was turning brown, starting to decay with the lack of sunlight, and it made for a powerful stench.

The steps were wide, about four feet at least, and they could both stand on the bottom step. Calvin lowered the boat hook into the water and it hit bottom at about eighteen inches. It wouldn't be over their heads, at least. They both heard a moan, and Emmet swung the light around. It came to rest on a steel cage, perched on a platform in the middle of the bunker. There was a man slumped in it.

"Dad!" Emmet shouted. Without thinking, he gave Apollo's leash to Calvin and plunged into the water, splashing his way toward the cage, determined to free his father. It didn't register that Apollo was barking like mad, nor did he hear or have time to react to Calvin's warning shout.

"Emmet, wait!"

Only a few feet separated him from the cage as he kicked through the grass and water, trying to reach it. "Dad!" he shouted again.

His shout was answered by a certain noise he'd heard before. At first it didn't register. Then it sounded again, drowning out Calvin's shouts of warning.

He heard something rise up out of the water behind him, and a leathery flapping sound. Surging forward, he tried to push it all out of his mind in order to reach his father.

But his path to the cage was cut off. One of the Pterogators popped out of the water in front of him, its long, birdlike neck writhing upward until its head was almost even with his. Its eyes, so like an owl's and looking out of place on the alligator-shaped head, stared at him with unadulterated menace. The mouth opened, revealing row upon row of razor-sharp teeth, and a chilling hiss came from somewhere deep in the creature's throat.

Emmet couldn't help himself.

He screamed. It felt like he was stuck in a tunnel of doom and the only thing in the noise and confusion surrounding him was Apollo's incessant barking and growling. Calvin's voice brought him back to reality.

"Emmet! Behind you! Duck!" Calvin shouted.

Emmet twisted around to find the other creature. This one was in the air, its limbs spread wide, gliding toward him. Emmet was surrounded, but he did what Calvin suggested, crouching at the waist. The hybrid in the air overshot him and nearly collided with the one to his front, instead crashing into the steel cage. The leathery sound he'd heard came from the winglike flaps of skin attached to its legs and sides.

He heard Calvin shouting and splashing toward him in the water, but didn't dare take his eyes off the monster in front of him. Calvin was yelling something about the flashlight, but Emmet thought clubbing the thing with a steel tube might just make it madder.

"Wedge it in its mouth!" Calvin shouted. He was almost to Emmet's side. The creature in front of him was eyeing Calvin like it hadn't eaten in weeks. It reared its head back on its long neck and the huge mouth opened again. Emmet estimated its mouth held roughly four thousand teeth. He held the flashlight out in front of him like a shield, thinking he was going to die in a stinky, alligator-infested swamp, and how mad that made him. He closed his eyes and waited for the end.

Something jolted his arm with a force that nearly knocked him backward. He staggered but didn't fall. The flashlight was torn from his grip, and he had to fight to stay on his feet. He opened his eyes to discover he was quite likely the luckiest human being on the planet at that particular moment.

The Pterogator staggered backward, shaking its head from side to side like Apollo might shake a rat. The Maglite, made of tungsten steel, was wedged in its mouth. It prevented it, for the moment at least, from closing its jaws. Emmet couldn't help it. He let out a yelp of triumph.

"Yeah!" he shouted. "How do you like me now, you stupid . . . stupid . . . gator-bird thing!"

The next thing he knew, Calvin was beside him. The second beast was still stunned from its collision with the cage, and it hung there, its claws wrapped in the mesh.

Calvin shoved the first-aid kit into Emmet's hands and as the creature hung there, he deftly maneuvered the boat hook over the top of its snout. The hook was solid steel, and bent into a half-circle shape, which made it easier to securely grasp ropes or poles when docking.

"What are you doing?" Emmet shouted, convinced now that Calvin had lost his mind. "Where's Apollo?" He looked at the steps and saw Apollo attached by his leash to a hook stuck in the concrete wall. The little mutt was trying to break the world record for angry barking.

"If it's like an alligator, the muscles to open its jaws are really weak. You can keep them closed with duct tape. But I don't have any duct tape, so this is going to have to do." He glanced over his shoulder at the other creature, which was now in the far corner of the bunker, still trying to dislodge the flashlight from its jaws.

"We've got to hurry," Calvin said. "He's handcuffed to the chair. A multi-tool is in my back pocket. Did I say hurry?"

Emmet reached into Calvin's back pocket and pulled out a metal tool with multiple blades, pliers, and other assorted implements. He rushed around to the other side of the cage. The door was held in place by a simple latch. He lifted it and scooted inside. He set the first-aid kit on the floor and went to work freeing his father.

"Dad!" He couldn't remember the last time he'd been this overjoyed. "I'm so happy to see you!"

"Happy later. Hurry now!" Calvin said. The creature was now wrestling a little bit and he struggled to keep its mouth closed with the boat hook.

Emmet gave his dad a quick once-over. He wore a few days' growth of beard, and his skin was pretty pale. He smelled and needed a shower, but he looked otherwise healthy. Emmet had no idea how to free him, though. The cuffs were solid steel.

"What's wrong?" Calvin asked through gritted teeth. The stunned Pterogator was recovering. He was using every bit of strength he needed to keep it at bay.

"It's the handcuffs! I don't suppose you have a handcuff key!" Emmet shouted.

"NO! Think of something!" Calvin said, fully occupied by wrangling the now thrashing creature.

Emmet looked around the cage. There was nothing he saw that would help. Then he looked at the chain. It wasn't that thick; maybe with the tool he could pry apart one of the links. He jammed the pliers into a link near his dad's wrist and pulled the handles apart. It wasn't working.

"What are you doing?" Calvin shouted.

"Trying . . ." Emmet put everything he had into it and pulled on the handles of the multi-tool with all his might. The link popped open.

"YES!" he shouted.

"Quicker would be better!" Calvin shouted. The noise of splashing, the creature's howls, and Apollo's indignation were overwhelming. Emmet's shout roused his father, who lifted his head and looked at him through cloudy eyes.

"Dad! Dad!" Emmet said. He slapped his father lightly on the cheek. He looked up when the cage rattled and he almost lost his balance. The Pterogator was really thrashing now. Calvin was struggling to keep it pinned against the cage with the boat hook. Its snout was flat against the steel mesh. But he wasn't going to be able to hold it for long.

Emmet looked down at the first-aid kit. He pulled it open and found a roll of medical tape.

"What are you doing? We've got to get out of here. Stop fooling around! I can't hold this thing much longer," Calvin said.

Emmet checked the location of the other beast: still swinging its head back and forth trying to dislodge the flashlight. He darted out of the cage and hurried around to where Calvin was trying to keep the creature pressed against the side of the cage.

"Hold it," Emmet said.

"What? No! Are you crazy?" Calvin said.

"Just a little bit longer!" Emmet yelled.

Calvin put all his weight into the hook, and pushed the creature's head against the cage. Emmet pulled on the tape and wrapped a long section around the mouth. It was sloppy and it wouldn't hold for long, but it would buy them some time.

"Okay," Emmet said. "Help me with my dad!"

"Good thinking," Calvin said. They rushed to the cage door. Emmet jammed the first-aid kit in his waistband and together they pulled Dr. Doyle through the door and to his feet. With one arm over each of their shoulders, they started toward the stairs. Apollo was nearly out of his mind to get to Dr. Doyle, and Emmet wondered if the leash would hold.

"Em . . . nut?" his dad mumbled.

"Yeah, Dad, it's me," Emmet said.

"Lots of bugs . . ." his dad mumbled.

"That's right, Dad, somebody drugged you. We've got you now. It's going to be okay," Emmet said, then turned to Calvin. "Keep an eye on that other one. I have no idea how long that tape will hold," Emmet said.

"No . . . Emnut . . . al . . . tors," his father croaked the words out.

"It's okay, Dad. We took care of them," Emmet said.

Emmet was sore and sweat was pouring down his face. The stairway seemed a thousand miles away and his father's legs were like rubber. But with each step, his confidence grew. Then he heard a loud cracking sound, and Calvin said, "Uh-oh!"

Emmet spared a second for a look behind them. The other Pterogator was finally free of the Maglite from its jaws. It opened its massive mouth and hissed. Tensing its muscles, it prepared to launch itself at them.

33

"**L**OOK OUT, CALVIN!" EMMET CRIED. NOT ONLY WERE the creatures strong, with big scary teeth, but the strength in their rear legs gave them enough power to launch themselves from the ground and glide over a short distance. All in all, Emmet would have been fine discovering this in a nature documentary, or by reading about it on the Internet, instead of witnessing it in person.

It leapt through the air with Calvin in its sights. The boat hook was no thicker than a broom handle, but Calvin swung it like a baseball bat. It connected with the critter's head and shattered, breaking into dozens of pieces. Calvin was left with a small pointed stick in his hands.

The creature was more surprised than injured by the blow. But it sank to the ground and backed away from Calvin, confused by his reaction. It opened its jaws and hissed, ready to launch another assault.

"Run, Emmet, get your dad out of here!" Calvin shouted.

"You've got to come . . ." Emmet couldn't get the words out before the beast's head shot forward and snapped at Calvin. To Emmet's complete surprise, he dodged out of the way. Calvin leapt on the creature's back, wrapping his arms around the snout. The Pterogator went mad with rage, shaking and twisting and writhing, but Calvin held on like a rodeo cowboy.

"Emmet . . . get . . . your . . . dad . . ." He couldn't finish. Instead, as the creature jumped around trying to throw him off, he jerked on the neck, bending it backward.

"Calvin, no! It's too strong! Run!" But Calvin didn't listen. With all his might, he pulled its neck farther back and the Pterogator settled, going to all fours, its neck bent at an odd angle. It thrashed again, then one final time, and went still. Calvin rolled forward so his body was holding the neck in place and quickly tore off his shirt, pulling it over the beast's head. He jumped up and ran to the stairs.

"Hurry," he said. He put Dr. Doyle's free arm over

his shoulder, unhooked Apollo, and wrapped the leash around his wrist. They scrambled their way up the stairs. The little dog was exhausted from barking and now merely huffed and growled, his body a tense ball of muscle.

"How did you . . . what did you . . . ?" Emmet was grunting with the effort.

"My uncles . . . at the Seminole reservation . . . taught me how . . ." They were halfway up the stairs. Dr. Doyle was like a dead weight and they were both nearly exhausted. ". . . to wrestle gators . . . you flip them over . . ."

"Pa' ou . . ." Dr. Doyle answered. He was blinking and shaking his head. Slowly he was waking up.

"What'd he say?" Emmet asked.

"They pass out," Calvin grunted.

"Why?"

"Can . . . we . . . discuss . . . later . . . ?" They could hear the creature with the taped mouth thrashing around below. Time to move.

"Hurry," Calvin said. Dr. Doyle's legs gained some life near the top. Emmet went through the hatch first, helping his dad climb out, with Calvin pushing him out from behind.

"The boat's right over here, Dad. We'll get you to the . . ."

"You won't get him anywhere," a voice said.

Standing between them and the canoe was a man dressed in a black jumpsuit, wearing a black ski mask covering all but his eyes.

He was also pointing a gun at them.

34

CALVIN TRIED PUSHING THE HATCH CLOSED.

"No!" Dr. Catalyst said. "Leave it open. We'll be joined by a couple of my greatest creations in a few seconds."

"They're dead," Calvin said. "Killed 'em."

"I doubt that," he said. "Not unless you had . . . well . . . what does it matter? You didn't have it."

"You must be Dr. Cat . . . sorry, what was it again?" Emmet asked.

The man's head swiveled until he focused on Emmet.

"Catalyst," he said, the gun pointed straight and level at Emmet's chest.

"Whatever," Emmet said.

No one said anything for a few seconds. Seeing the man who did this to his father made Emmet feel like he was standing outside himself. All the emotions of the past year and a half were boiling up inside him and it seemed like they were coming out of his ears. His vision darkened and in his mind he was somewhere else watching a cartoon version of the Emmet he thought he knew.

" 'Whatever'?" Dr. Catalyst said. "Surely that can't be all you have to say. What did you think of my creations?"

"Your creations? What are you talking about? Those mini-dinosaurs? Not much," Emmet said.

Dr. Catalyst chuckled. "I hardly think that's the case. Magnificent, aren't they?"

"They're magnificent at sucking," Emmet said. "Heck, Calvin wrestled one of them with one arm and turned its brain to jelly, and I took care of the other one with some tape. That's right. I said tape. Some big creations. Both of them beat up by a couple of kids who don't even have cell phones yet." He looked at his dad, who he really wished would wake up all the way and think of something.

"By the way, Dad, how come I don't have a cell phone?" he said. He turned his face away from Dr. Catalyst, toward his father and Calvin. As he did, he raised his eyebrows at Calvin.

Dr. Catalyst was silent a moment. It was hard for Emmet to get a read on him because he couldn't see his face. Only his eyes, peering through the slit in the hood, gave any indication of his identity. They were dark brown.

"Funny. I've only just met you and already I've had enough of your mouth, boy," Dr. Catalyst said. The gun was still pointing at Emmet's chest.

Emmet tried to think of something, anything to get them out of this mess. The sun was coming up over the horizon now, and all he could think of was to keep Dr. Catalyst talking. Then Dr. Geaux would find out he and Calvin were missing and send the cavalry. But that could still be a while. His only option was trying to keep Dr. Catalyst riled up and hope he made some kind of mistake.

"My mouth? And truthfully, 'Dr. Catalyst,' what kind of name is that? I mean, I've seen your little Internet videos, and by the way, the videos of little kittens getting stuck in boxes are way more entertaining, but you make yourself out to be some kind of environmental supervillain and the best you can come up with is 'Dr. Catalyst'? If you're going to stick with the dopey name, you should at least get a cape or a better costume," Emmet said. "This ninja look is so 1990s."

"What are you doing?" Calvin whispered.

"Shh. It's all part of my plan," Emmet said.

"The get-us-killed plan?" Calvin whispered back.

"No, the other one . . ."

"Shut up! Stop talking, both of you," Dr. Catalyst shouted at them. "The two of you have ruined everything. Years of work. Hundreds of thousands of dollars of —"

"Two words," Emmet interrupted him. "Boo. Hoo. You kidnapped my dad, you big gob of spit!"

"I wasn't . . ." Dr. Catalyst started to say, but was stopped by the sight and sound of the creatures roaring out of the hatch. Calvin jumped behind Emmet and Dr. Doyle, with a shout of surprise. As he did, quick as a flash, he pulled his cell phone out of his pocket, pushed the button for the ranger station, and dropped it into the grass at his feet. Emmet saw it all. He just hoped Dr. Catalyst hadn't. And that the phone picked up a signal.

Apollo, who was straining at the leash, trying to get at Dr. Catalyst and tear him apart with all twenty pounds of his righteous indignation, turned his attention to the creatures. He found his voice and started barking again. Loudly. The creatures landed on the ground and stared back at the mutt.

Slowly they edged away from the Pterogators, who were staring back and forth at each other, the three of them, and Dr. Catalyst. Emmet thought the two ugly critters might be voting on which one of them to eat first. One had pieces of tape hanging from its snout; it had managed to break through somehow. The other one still looked a little sluggish. The boys kept moving, holding up Emmet's dad, who for some reason appeared to have gone back to sleep. It must have been a strong drug in his system.

"Stop right there!" Dr. Catalyst commanded. He kept the gun pointed in their general direction, but his attention was now divided between his hybrids and the three of them.

The creatures lifted their necks and stared back at him now. There was something in the movement that just gave Emmet the creeps.

"'Birs . . . 'hine . . ." Dr. Doyle muttered, raising his head, his face twisted in concentration as he tried to will the drugs to wear off.

"What did you give my dad? He's usually a lot more chatty than this," Emmet demanded.

"He's fine . . . will be . . . would have been fine, if you hadn't interfered," Dr. Catalyst said. Emmet stared at him, but his eyes kept darting toward the creatures.

"Em . . . nut . . . birs . . . 'jjjiny . . ." Dr. Doyle could barely speak. But to Emmet it sounded like he'd said "Emmet. Birds. Heiny." He was gaga. There weren't any birds around and it was no time to be making jokes.

"What did he say?" Calvin whispered.

"I don't —"

Then Emmet remembered something! He'd been out in the field with his father when they'd lived in Texas a few years ago. They were watching prairie hawks diving from high up in the sky, and his dad had talked about the acute vision of raptors — birds of prey.

They, like most birds, were attracted to shiny objects, his dad said. Could his dad be trying to tell him something he'd figured out about the creatures?

"Sorry, Dad," Emmet said. He knew his father was trying to say something important, but he didn't know what. "I'm not sure what you mean. . . ."

"Shut up, I said! Stop talking. I need to think. . . ." Dr. Catalyst was worried now, and trying hard not to show it.

Emmet watched the hybrids waddling back and forth at the hatch entrance. Apollo was nearly yanking Calvin's arm off and his barking was starting to irritate the creatures. Apollo acted as if he couldn't decide what he wanted to bite first.

Half bird. Half alligator, he thought.

"Em . . . 'jiny . . . on . . . 'atlyst." His dad was trying hard to stand up, but he was weak and tired. His muscles wouldn't work right. Even so, he was trying to move himself in front of Emmet and Calvin, but they held him in place.

"You better let us go!" Calvin said. "My mom is out looking for us. She'll be here any minute."

Emmet whispered, "Really? 'My mom'? That's going to scare him? 'My mom will beat you up'? Why don't . . ."

Then it came to Emmet. He still carried the first-aid kit, which was inside a thin, folding metal box. He pulled it out and turned it over in his hand. The rising sun reflected off it, and the glare flashed on the ground at his feet. He moved it along the ground until it flashed in the eyes of the closest hybrid. It blinked and opened its mouth and roared.

Emmet changed the angle of the shiny first-aid kit until the reflection blinked on Dr. Catalyst's arm, the one holding the gun. The hybrid's eyes followed the reflection like a cat follows one of those little red dots from a laser pointer. It roared a few more times and Emmet wiggled the box. The light dazzled, also catching the attention of Dr. Catalyst, who was busy thinking about his next move.

"What are you doing? Drop that box . . ." But he didn't get a chance to finish. The hybrid crouched and leapt, spreading its limbs, its mouth open. Dr. Catalyst let out a scream of agonizing pain as the creature bit down on his arm.

He dropped the gun.

35

EVERYTHING HAPPENED FAST, BUT TO EMMET IT FELT like they were moving in slow motion.

"Calvin, the gun!" Emmet shouted.

Calvin scrambled forward, plucked the gun from the grass, and heaved it into the swamp.

"Why did you do that? I wanted you to shoot these things," Emmet cried.

"Don't know how to shoot," Calvin said. He rushed back to help move Dr. Doyle toward the boat.

"Seriously? You wrestle alligators and pilot an airboat but you don't know how to shoot?"

"My mom doesn't like guns." He shrugged when he said it. Quickly he got Dr. Doyle's arm back over his shoulder and tried to calm Apollo, which was impossible. Emmet was afraid the poor dog might pass out.

"Easy, Apollo," he said. But it had no effect. The dog was clearly annoyed that he was not being allowed to attack something.

They tried to move quickly. Dr. Catalyst was screaming, "Get it off me! Get it off me!"

"Should we help him?" Calvin asked.

"Not a chance!" Emmet said. "I've got my dad. You keep an eye on the other one, hold on to Apollo, and get the boat ready."

The canoe was only a few yards away, but it seemed like miles. Dr. Doyle's legs were still not fully working. Behind him, he could hear Dr. Catalyst screaming.

"Uh-oh!" Calvin said.

"I hate when you say that!" Emmet said.

"It's gone!"

"What's gone?"

"The other gator-thingy," Calvin said.

"How can it . . . ?" A shadow flashed on the ground in front of Emmet. "Heads up!" he shouted.

They ducked, and Emmet couldn't hold his dad up anymore. They tumbled to the ground. The Pterogator screeched as it floated over them, landing on the ground and cutting off their route to the boat.

"I really hate these things," Emmet said.

"Try circling around it," Calvin said. He helped Emmet pull Dr. Doyle to his feet. The creature studied them. Dr. Catalyst's Internet videos said the creatures he created only fed on snakes, but right then it looked more than ready to try something new on the menu.

They went to their left and it moved with them. When they tried to go right, it hopped in front of them again.

Dr. Catalyst had stopped screaming. Emmet kept his eyes on the monster. "Do you see Dr. Catalyst?" he asked.

Calvin looked around. "No, he . . ." They heard an airboat fan start up and come to full power, the noise lessening as it got farther away.

"He's getting away!" Calvin said.

"He won't get far. Probably only has half an arm. We've got bigger problems," Emmet said.

They didn't have any weapons. The giant Pterogator in front of them watched their movements, head bobbing in concert with each step they took. It leapt in the air toward them. This time, Emmet tossed the first-aid kit, hitting it in the eye before it could snatch one of them. It squealed and landed off to the side.

With the path cleared, they made tracks for the canoe, helping Dr. Doyle to lie down inside between the bench seats. Emmet took the leash for Apollo, who jumped into the boat and went immediately to work cleaning

Dr. Doyle's face. Calvin untied the rope and got them ready to launch.

"Uh-oh!" Calvin said.

"Please stop saying that! I'm begging you," Emmet said.

But then Emmet saw what Calvin did. The hybrid landed on the bow of the canoe. It stood on its hind legs and roared. Emmet was so wishing for a cannon.

"Here!" Calvin shouted. Emmet looked back as Calvin tossed him a small fire extinguisher from where it was bolted next to the electric engine. That Calvin. Always prepared.

"Are you kidding!"

"Do it! Now!" Calvin said. He flipped the switch and the motor hummed to life. The giant beast was rocking the canoe as it beat its leathery winglike flaps. Emmet scrambled forward to get in front of his dad, who was still lying on his back. He pointed the plastic barrel of the fire extinguisher at the ugly thing's face and pulled the trigger. Foam shot out, covering it like white shaving cream.

It made a noise that sounded like a sneeze, shaking its head from side to side. All Emmet could do was hope the other one wasn't around. The foam flew as the creature whipped its neck back and forth. Emmet nearly shouted with joy as the creature tumbled off the bow. The engine powered up and Calvin backed the canoe into the swamp.

Turning the tiller, he steered the canoe in the opposite direction and gave it all the power the electric motor had. The small island receded behind them. The sun was now over the trees and Emmet could see the creatures standing on the shore, confused and angry. But pretty soon they couldn't see them at all.

They had made it.

36

DR. GEAUX TRIED TO CONVINCE EMMET TO COME BACK to their house for the night. He refused, and stayed in the hospital with his dad. She insisted that the Florida City police post guards outside the room. There had been a large explosion in the swamp, and her team discovered what looked to be the remains of a concrete bunker and pieces of lab equipment.

Dr. Catalyst might have disappeared. Or he might still be out there, she told Calvin. They found a high-tech camouflaged airboat abandoned in the swamp. It was covered in a lot of blood. Their working theory was that after Dr. Catalyst fled the island, he returned to his lab and set off pre-wired explosives. In his escape attempt he was most likely overcome by blood loss. He probably fell into the swamp. His body was yet to be recovered.

Dr. Geaux wasn't too mad about Emmet and Calvin slipping out to search. Emmet explained to her how he'd gotten the idea in science class to look for cold spots instead of heat signatures. She'd told him most of the animals migrated out of the park because of the hybrids. Emmet reminded her of his theory about how someone doing what Dr. Catalyst was doing must be in the swamp. But he wouldn't want excess heat to give him away.

Finding cold spots in the swamp, where Dr. Catalyst insulated his compounds against the heat sensors, had proven to be the right approach. The swamp gave off heat from the decaying plants and animals, and even rocks warmed by the sun during the day would still give off some residual heat to an infrared sensor. Calvin had told Emmet that Plantation Row probably once had power. And Emmet had looked for big cold spots nearest the old homes.

"Why didn't you come to me?" Dr. Geaux asked him.

"I'm sorry. I should have. But I went on my own. Calvin followed me —"

"And he and I are going to have a big, long talk about that," Dr. Geaux interrupted him.

"Yes. Right. My bad. I'm sure he was just checking up on me. I totally talked him into taking me out into the swamp. It wasn't pretty. I begged, actually. It's my fault. He shouldn't get in trouble," Emmet said.

Dr. Geaux gave a big fake sigh and laughed. "Men!" she said. "All right. You stay here tonight, but you let your dad rest, okay?"

Emmet sighed when she left. They had just gotten lucky and found his dad at the first spot. Despite her mild annoyance, she had admitted to him it was pretty good thinking.

Emmet woke up in a chair to the sound of his dad calling his name.

"Hey, pal," Dr. Doyle croaked. His voice was still thick and raspy.

"Dad!" Emmet came awake and launched himself to his father's bedside. He hugged him like he would never let him go. "When you're feeling better, I'm going to kill you," Emmet said in mock anger.

"Then it's a good thing the doctor said I'm in for a long recovery," Dr. Doyle said.

"He didn't say that. The doctor said you'll be fine in a couple of days. Then we're going to have a chat," Emmet said, teasing. He stayed there at his dad's side. He finally felt good again. Untangled.

"Rosalita told me some of what you did. I don't

remember all of it, but maybe I'm the one who should have a chat with you," his dad said, smiling.

"Whatever," Emmet said. "Did you know Calvin wrestles alligators?"

"Yes. His mom told me. He spends time with his family on the reservation every summer. It's a Seminole tradition."

"He's a pretty cool kid," Emmet said.

"Sounds like it."

"Dad, how did you think to tell me about shiny objects when we were out there? It saved us."

"I don't remember a lot of it. The only thing I knew was someone wanted to hurt you. My arms and legs couldn't move, and I felt helpless. Birds are attracted to light. Dr. Catalyst made these things by recombining DNA. Alligators will strike at fish when their scales flash in the sun. It was probably just my training coming to the fore and me hoping for anything that might save you," he said. His voice was getting weaker, and Emmet knew he needed to rest.

"You and your science," Emmet said.

Dr. Doyle's eyes were starting to droop. But he chuckled softly.

"What's so funny?"

"You're always getting on me about 'science,'" his dad said. "Look who used science to find me."

"Yeah . . . whatever . . . next time you are on your own."

His dad squeezed his hand and drifted off to sleep.

Emmet had more questions. But they could wait. With his dad asleep, he had time to think. Dr. Catalyst had gone to a lot of trouble and expense to launch his little crusade. And despite everything, the blown-up lab, the abandoned airboat, and all the rest, Emmet still had that tickling feeling crawling across the back of his neck and shoulders. A man so driven and consumed by his cause would have backup plans for his backup plans.

He went to the window and opened the blinds, letting a little light into the room. After his time in the dark, dank bunker, he found he was getting fond of the Florida sunshine. Staring out the window, he saw an osprey far off in the distance circling high in the sky over the Everglades.

Dr. Catalyst was still out there somewhere. Emmet was sure of it.

Epilogue

DEEP IN THE DARKEST, MOST REMOTE PART OF THE Everglades, the full moon hung low over the swamp. The sky looked like spilled ink and the bright moonlight obscured the stars, for now. Spanish moss hung like cobwebs from the cypress and mangrove trees, and the chirping frogs were silent for once.

There was a stranger in their midst.

On a high branch in a twisted mangrove tree, a nest of twigs, grass, and mud was wedged between two branches. It was a big nest, and the other animals of the swamp gave it a wide berth. No birds landed in the tree, no possums or raccoons frolicked nearby. They were afraid of what resided there.

Nails sat atop it, all of her senses alert. Something was coming. An intruder, perhaps out of curiosity, or driven mad by hunger, was somewhere nearby. Nails sniffed the air. It was a snake.

She gave a bellowing call, and her tiny offspring, who were climbing and exploring the branches of the tree, came skittering back to the nest. Like her alligator relatives, she lowered her head, opened her mouth, and the small babies who looked like her in every way climbed inside. She gently closed her jaws and waited.

The python was nearly twenty feet long. It slithered down from a branch above and peered at Nails, its tongue flicking, working the air. The serpent could not figure out what she was exactly, but it had not fed in days. There were still unhatched eggs in the nest, and those would make a tasty meal.

Dr. Catalyst had made a grievous error in his research. His experiments had recombined DNA, resequenced genes, and used a variety of different growth hormones to create the Pterogators. He thought his creatures could never reproduce. But nature is not static. Survival in any species is paramount. And the change in his creatures that began with the subject recovered by Dr. Geaux had continued with Hammer and Nails. Eventually, even a cloned species will adapt, and change. Such instinct is encoded in the DNA of every species. Dr. Catalyst had been sloppy and let his ego and naiveté color his judgment. Now he and the swamp he sought to protect would pay a horrible price.

Nails hissed through her nostrils, but could not open her mouth for fear of losing a baby. With her forepaws she rolled the remaining eggs further beneath her. The snake moved closer.

It reared back, ready to strike, when the nest shook with a violent impact. The snake's attack died in mid-air. Hammer arrived. Gliding to the nest from his perch nearby, he landed claws-first on the python, which now twisted upward trying to find a way free from the deadly grasp of the beast holding it.

But it was too late. Hammer's neck flew back, jaws open, and with one bite, the snake died and went still. Nails hissed through her nostrils, and Hammer glided away to his perch, but not before swallowing a large chunk of meat.

When he was gone, Nails lowered her head to the floor of the nest and opened her mouth. Her babies burst out, momentarily confused and disoriented. They were less than a week old, and already nearly six inches in length. Eight of them survived the first hatching.

Each one hesitated a moment, until the smell of the

dead snake reached them. They made small *skree skree* sounds and clamored across the floor of the nest, crawling onto the carcass of the snake, where they began to methodically devour it.

It was dinnertime.

FROM DR. CATALYST'S FILES

"Pterogator"

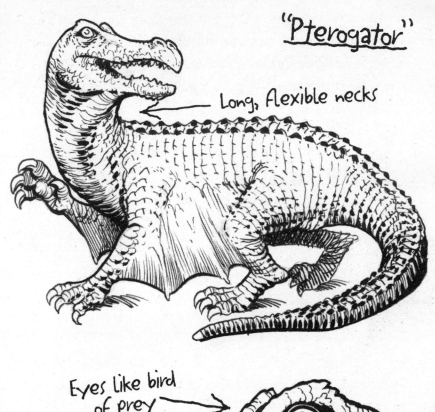

Long, flexible necks

Eyes like bird of prey

Deadly claws — CAUTION!
Very sharp!

Wing flaps
allow gliding

WATCH FOR THE NEXT
KILLER SPECIES

SCHOOL IS OUT AND SUMMER HAS ARRIVED. AFTER FOILING Dr. Catalyst, Emmet was hoping he and his father might be able to return to Montana. But working to undue the damage already caused by Dr. Catalyst is a big job. And now Dr. Doyle has been permanently assigned to Everglades National Park. Instead of heading west as he hoped, Emmet grouses about spending a summer in the hot, humid Florida sun.

But it isn't just a longing for the mountains that pulls at Emmet. He can't rid himself of the feeling that Dr. Catalyst is out there somewhere. Everyone else believes that he died in the swamp or that he's finished and hiding away somewhere licking his wounds. But Emmet doesn't think someone so committed to his cause would give up so easily. And the occasional nightmares of the fearsome Pterogators Dr. Catalyst created aren't helping him any.

To celebrate the start of summer, Dr. Geaux and Dr. Doyle take Emmet, Calvin, and their friends to a nearby cove for snorkeling. The water is warm and crystal clear, but the reef below them is swarming with Lionfish . . . and devoid of other sea life. Emmet learns that much like the pythons and boa constrictors of the Everglades, the Lionfish are another invasive species that are devastating the marine ecosystem.

Then, without warning, a group of odd fish appear from the depths of the cove. They look like a cross between the great barracuda and the moray eel, and they begin quickly devouring the lionfish right before the kids' eyes. These strange creatures are big, fast, and have mouths full of razor-sharp teeth. Emmet starts to get an eerie feeling. The speed and strength of the fish are almost unnatural.

The creatures also have voracious appetites. After clearing the reef of Lionfish in a matter of minutes, they soon turn their attention to Emmet and his friends. All Emmet's worries about Dr. Catalyst suddenly take a backseat as the strange fish begin heading straight for them. Right now he's only got one thing on his mind.

Survival.

From bestselling author
Kathryn Lasky

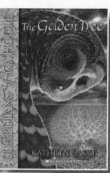